TENNESSEE BOY

TENNESSEE BOY

by GLORIA ROOT SAVOLDI

THE WESTMINSTER PRESS
Philadelphia

ISBN 0-664-32513-0

LIBRARY OF CONGRESS CATALOG CARD No. 76-185927

PUBLISHED BY THE WESTMINSTER PRESS®
PHILADELPHIA, PENNSYLVANIA
PRINTED IN THE UNITED STATES OF AMERICA

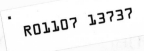
Library of Congress Cataloging in Publication Data

Savoldi, Gloria Root.
  Tennessee boy.

  SUMMARY: In 1865 two thirteen-year-old boys, one black, one white, discover many things about each other and the war while traveling from the Tennessee mountains to Washington City.
  [1. Friendship—Fiction. 2. United States—History—Civil War—Fiction] I. Title.
PZ7.S267Te   76-185927
ISBN 0-664-32513-0

          jS
         268
          te

For my husband, Frank

1

CLAY GATLIN stood in the doorway of his cabin and looked out across the windswept ridge that was his home in the Great Smoky Mountains.

He was tall for thirteen, skinny as a scrub pine, and his hands big-knuckled and red from the February cold. He turned to his hound dog hunched beside the spluttering fire and said, "Look at that fire spit, Bory. That means they'll come a fresh snow tonight."

The hound burrowed his nose in overlapping forepaws.

Clay drew on his Pa's Confederate coat and went outside for firewood. He walked in free-swinging, long strides until he came to the woodpile against the mule shed. As he walked, he pushed the arms of the coat higher so his hands could be free.

His Pa, wounded at Knoxville and come home to die, had left Clay the coat—which was a butternut rather than a true gray—his hunting rifle, a battered canteen, a nicked ambrotype of Clay's grandmother, the mule Lazy Girl, a two-wheeled plow, and the cabin. The cabin wasn't much, Clay reflected, starting back with an armload, but his heart swelled with pride when he looked at it.

The cabin, built at a long-ago "log raising," sat proud and snug at the top of the ridge.

Notched logs, cut at the proper turn of the moon, fit together so nice they didn't need much chinking. Set among protecting pine, hemlock, silver bell, and cherry, dark blue wisps curling from its chimney, the cabin reminded Clay of a picture his big brother, Clem, brought him once from a trinket store in Knoxville.

Inside, he banged the door tight and bolted it, then turned his attention to supper. His keen blue eyes quickly took in the dwindling supplies—some sassafras chips, a string of pumpkin rings, white cornmeal, a jar of beets put up in the fall, a half jug of sorghum molasses, long ropes of shucky beans hanging from the smoke-blackened ceiling, and a small piece of salt pork wrapped in blue homespun.

Foraging soldiers had captured the wild pigs, so there was little meat that winter. Just the piece of salt pork no bigger than a man's fist.

He opened the cellar door beneath his feet and brought up a small crock of goat's milk that his good neighbor John Brewster had toted from the next ridge two days before. He touched some to his tongue. It was still sweet, so he poured a little into an iron pot that swung over the fire.

Whimpering softly, the dog rose to his feet and watched, heavy-lidded.

"All right, Bory," Clay said, "I'll give you a mite."

He poured some of the milk into a tin for Beauregard and watched the dog slurp it up. The dog's snuff-colored coat was lusterless and his ribs stuck out.

Clay rubbed the dog's nose and talked to him gently, all the while stroking his ears. "Don't worry, Old Bory, we'll go out in the morning to check the trap line. And if they's fresh snow, we'll go tracking. Maybe we'll get you a nice fat possum. Or a squirrel." Clay could almost imagine deer tracks, but he couldn't let his hankering get the best of him.

The dog, seeming to understand, went back to his place by the hearth.

Clay's own stomach rumbled as he added water and cooked up a mess of beans in the same pot that had warmed the milk. He eyed the piece of salt pork.

His mouth, remembering the taste, watered.

Slowly, carefully, he sliced a thin piece of the pork and laid it in the pot to simmer with the beans. After a while he served up some of the vittles in Bory's tin and gulped down the rest himself. Then he took a piece of corn pone, left from breakfast, and wiped the pot clean. He ate part of this and gave the rest to Bory.

Clay sat in the squeaky rocker by the fire and watched sparks shoot onto the rough flooring. Outside, the wind howled around the ridge and complained beneath the shallow eaves.

Sitting by the warmth of the fire, Clay thought sharply of his Pa. Pa had sure favored this time of day. His chores finished, he would sit beside his well-laid fire listening to the churning, whistling winds and say, contentedly, how this was his "thinkin' time," his favorite time of day.

In the spring, when fire cherry, trillium, and raspberry spilled their colors over the mountains, Pa would go outside and meditate. In his straight-back chair he would settle near the edge of the ridge and watch point after point roll away. His back still sore from plowing, he would tilt back, bare feet on a gum tree, and watch the smoky veil of mist ripple and change and shift. Until darkness covered him over.

Sometimes Pa would pull a mouth organ from his pocket

9

and roll a song for Clay and his brothers. His Ma would come out of the cabin, wiping dishwater on her apron, and stand beside Pa.

Pa told stories, too, summer and winter. He taught them the millions of things his Pa had taught him, and his Pa before. Clay knew they'd sink to beggar trash in no time if they hadn't learnt from their Pa so well.

"Plant potatoes in the dark of the moon so they won't have too many eyes . . . If you'll mark the bottom of your churn with a cross, the butter will come quicker . . .

"Strangers ain't never to be trusted . . . always plant peppers when you're good and mad at your wife . . . and give your gourds a hard cussin' or they won't come up."

Pa told them about the Indians too. He told how the Chickasaw and the Cherokees padded through the ridges on the train of bison and how the trappers used to come for trade with the Cherokee. He showed them a tomahawk dent on the side of the cabin beside the chimney, and an arrowhead scar near the door.

Clay sighed. It didn't seem fittin' that Pa was out there behind the cabin where the little crosses stood in their family burying ground—him that loved to work hard and sing songs and laugh and tell stories. Him that knew every leaf on every tree. And every flower and critter hereabouts.

Ma was out there, too, next to Pa. Clay had peeled the little cross of pine himself and seen that she was laid away proper. When the fever took her, last fall, and after her it took little Davey, he'd seen everything was done like Ma would have wanted.

Sometimes he was fairly sure he'd bust inside, thinking about them. Pa. Ma. Little Davey with his fair hair and easy laugh. But they were together and the neighbors had come from the other ridges and brought the preacher feller and he said some fine words.

Pete, the eldest, was lost at Chickamauga and Ma never got over it, while she lived, that Pete couldn't be buried in the little family plot behind the cabin.

Him and Clem were the only two Gatlins left, the only two to carry on the Gatlin name.

He tried not to think of Clem up there with General Wright's unit guarding Washington City where the Yankee president lived. Clem, wearing the blue to the everlasting shame of his Pa's memory.

Clem.

Sometimes Clay said the name in a dream and sometimes he felt in his bones that he had to get to Washington City to see Clem and to tell him about Ma and Pa.

Pa had crossed out Clem's name in the big family Bible. "Forget that boy," Pa used to say whenever him or Ma would mention Clem's name. "That fly-up-the-creek is no-count. Marrying that girl in Knoxville and traipsing up north with her. Then joining up with the Bluebirds when the war was commenced. He ain't a Gatlin no more. Never speak his name." Pa was sure stubborn.

His brother was always kind to Clay, though, bringing him presents from Knoxville and helping with the wood-chopping and teaching him how to trap. Of all his brothers, Clem was the one he favored. No matter how Pa had felt about him, Clay still kept a secret, special place in his heart for Clem. Clay could fairly see him now—his handsome face all smiles and windburned, wearing his floppy cinnamon-colored hat with the wide brim. Eyes so snapping and blue they reminded Clay of a jay's twinkling wing.

Restless, Clay got up from his rocker and laid another log on the fire. A spitting fire, according to mountain tradition, meant there would come a big snow. So Clay listened to the fire spitting and to the wind whining, and he knew in his bones it would be snowing outside.

11

"Tomorrow morning we'll go tracking," he said sleepily to Beauregard. "Maybe we can fill up our larder."

He heard a far-off rumbling and he reckoned that some oak had crashed on the mountainside.

The thundering lingered in his mind a spell and he thought of the rumbling and thundering of cannons. He'd never been close to the fighting, but Pete had sent letters that Ma had read, telling about the big war cannons. Pa, too, had told how they boomed "like the crashin' of forest trees."

Clay was just eight and a half years old when the fighting had commenced. Later, after Chickamauga Creek and Knoxville, he had begged his Ma to let him join the boys in gray.

He was only eleven when he had asked her, but he had reckoned he was tall for his age and maybe they'd teach him to be a drummer boy. He'd heard about a lot of boys eleven and twelve who bravely beat the drums in battle.

"Clay Gatlin," his Ma had threatened, "if you speak another word about such foolishness, I'll whup you till you can't sit for a month of Sundays."

He heard his Ma cry that night, and he knew he must never mention it again. As she lay with the fever she had made him promise he would never try to join the fighting.

Even now he knew that if he tried to join the battle, his Ma's spirit would surely come back and haunt him.

The Rebs were dug in now at a place in Virginia called Petersburg. And Jeff Davis was safe up in the capital at Richmond. Yet John Brewster had told Clay that Jeff Davis was not safe for long—and that the days of the war were surely numbered.

"Why, can't drag on more than a month or so," said his neighbor on his last visit. "Sherman's bummers has ruined everything in Georgia, and Hood was licked bad in

12

Nashville. Why, you should see the slaves leaving the plantations, following them Union boys up north. I tell you, Clay, they're pulling out so fast there soon won't be a field hand left in the whole blamed South!

"Most of 'em," Brewster said, "are going to Washington City." He laughed and slapped his thigh. "Why, they think Lincoln freed them all personal!"

Clay knew that John Brewster had taught himself book learning and he respected his judgment. But he found it hard to believe that the South had already lost the fight. He felt indescribably sad, because he remembered his Pa arguing with Yankee sympathizers, telling them, "We might not share board and ways with them that owns slaves to work their lands, but Tennessee is part of the South. We was born South, and we'll die if we have to, fighting for the Gray."

Clay knew that most of his neighbors sympathized with the Union. His Ma had told him his Pa was a brave man to hold to his Southern sympathies. "But your Pa's like that," she'd say, not trying to hide her pride. "He always speaks up for the way he believes—even if he ain't liked for it."

As the war progressed, and Clay occasionally visited Knoxville or Findlay's Store at the foot of the mountain, he had learned how bands of east Tennesseans had burned railroad bridges to help the Unionists, and how they had "kicked up all kinds of trouble" against the Rebs. He wondered that his Pa could hold so strong to his own beliefs and still live peaceable among his neighbors.

He was proud of his Pa for his stubbornness. He was a Reb, too, like his Pa.

John Brewster had explained to Clay that many of the mountain folk didn't cotton to the big plantation owners and those other "uppity" folk that looked down on the ridgemanites, or mountain people. Yet, his Pa had hoped the South would win. He had often exclaimed, eyes wide and blue like Clem's and snapping with merriment, "When them Yankees see the whites of our eyes, they'll take to the woods like treed possums!"

Clay didn't think much about the meaning of the war. As to slavery, they'd never had slaves in these mountains, but he'd heard that great fields of "southern snow," or cotton, rolled away to the west of Knoxville, and wealthy "covites" that farmed in the river bottomland used them by the hundreds.

He had a bitter resentment for the colored folk. If it wasn't for them, there wouldn't be a war in the first place. And if it wasn't for the war, his Pa would still be here and Pete wouldn't have spilled his blood at Chickamauga.

As the fire died, Clay sidled up closer to Old Bory and wrapped a patchwork quilt around himself, Indian fashion. He was too cold to leave the fire and crawl into bed.

2

NEXT MORNING BEFORE SUNUP, Clay pushed back a drift of fresh snow, forcing open the cabin door. In the watery light he could see a thin white blanket over the shed, and the trees, beyond, were powdered to a blue-white sheen.

He breathed deep of the icy air and it bit into his lungs.

"See, Bory, you can't argufy with a spitting fire. Come on, boy, let's get that stubborn mule some vittles. Then we'll check the line."

Lazy Girl looked at them with languid eyes and an indifferent flick of her tail as Clay threw hay in her stall. Clay patted her flanks, which were dull from winter, then called to Beauregard, who ran after him. As he scampered down the ridge toward the first trap, Clay carried his flintlock.

As always, he felt a heady sense of adventure when he neared the gully beside the icy blue-tinted stream where the first trap lay. He began to hanker for game stew, and this made him quicken his step. Bory beat him to the trap by at least thirty paces, and an excited yelp told him they'd bagged something.

Clay watched his warm breath whiten the air as he hurried to the trap. He came upon it then, and a rabbit lay limp upon the snow.

"Well, Bory, if we ain't fetched us a rabbit! A mite skinny, but it'll stew up fine. You hold off while I pry open this trap."

Clay opened the steel jaws, plunked the dead rabbit in his shoulder sling, then reset the trap. Pulling himself out of the gully, he saw that Beauregard had already headed for the bigger trap down by the granddaddy oak. Bory knew each trap in the line.

He usually yelped, high-pitched, as if to tell Clay he had beat him again. But this time he was whimpering. It was a soft whimper, low in his throat. Then a growl. A warning.

Clay's pulse quickened.

"Bory! Why you taking on so?"

As he neared the trap, his fingers tightened on his rifle.

When he got close, Clay could make out something lying under a light snow blanket, partly covered. He saw a dark hand stretched out. A shoulder in a thick brown coat, a haversack strapped to the shoulder. A man's head, face-down. Clay's trap tightly imprisoned the man's foot, just above the ankle. A frozen strip of blanket showed dark bloodstains.

Clay sucked in his breath when he looked back to the dark hand, which was almost the color of a buckeye. *A runaway slave!*

He bent over the still figure. Cautiously. Slowly. Then he snapped back. What would a slave be doing way up here? Maybe others traveled with him. Maybe a whole band of them, foraging.

Clay looked around. The only footsteps in the snow, now faint, but unmistakable, stumbled in a zigzag line to the trap.

If others were with him, there would be other tracks. Clay's cold fingers tightened again on the rifle. He wanted to get away from this place, back to the warm haven of his

16

cabin. He didn't hanker for trouble. Bory, still growling, circled and recircled the prone figure, sniffing furiously.

Clay couldn't make out if the man was alive or not. Half afraid to find out, he poked him with the end of his rifle. When the figure in the snow did not move, Clay bent closer. Quickly, then, fighting the fear and grudging curiosity that rose in his breast, Clay grabbed the half-frozen form by the shoulders and turned it over.

He sucked in his breath. "Why! It's a young boy!"

He bent closer. It was a scuff of a boy who looked to be about nine or ten, with a small round face and a dark-red woolly cap pulled down to the eyebrows. He was still breathing, but from the hollows beneath the closed eyes, a body could see that he was half starved. On his hands were patches of dried blood like summer berry stains. And the nails were broken.

A long sword gleamed dully by the boy's side. It was almost as long as the boy himself.

The sun, cold and distant, started to rise in the sky, and everything was suddenly dipped in pink and gold. Clay wondered, from studying his misty breath, how cold it was. It was certainly cold. He had no way of knowing how long the boy had lain there, whether frostbite had started to set in. It didn't appear he'd lost much blood. Clay knew, though, that when the wind was up and it was cold, like today, a body could get frostbite and it could be killing.

He scowled. He didn't want to fool with no stranger. Especially a runaway slave. His familiar hatred, bitter, maybe unreasoning, yet strong in his senses like a sickness, told him to leave the boy where he was. It wasn't his fault that the boy had stumbled into his trap. None of his business at all.

On the heels of that thought came the feeling, just as strong, that it was his trap that bit now into the boy's flesh.

17

He could not ignore that. He thought, too, of the words in the Good Book. He thought of his Ma, reading the words to him, firelight flickering over her kindly face. What would Ma have him do? She'd always taught him to be a good Samaritan.

Clay flung a look back toward the cabin above him. He couldn't make it out from there through the thick evergreens, but he could see the thin line of smoke rising to the morning sky. A wintering cardinal cut a blazing path across the sky.

Clay felt as small as a blade of grass.

If he took the boy to his cabin, no telling what he'd do if he got the chance. Maybe he'd try to run him through with that sword, or hit him over the head with something when he wasn't looking. No use asking for trouble.

That boy sure looked like the hind wheels of bad luck. He might be desperate, like some animal.

Clay hesitated. His inbred mountain caution made him steel every muscle. He wanted to leave the boy there, to forget he'd found him. Leave him to Providence.

Still . . .

Cursing himself for his softness, he pried open the trap and freed the boy's leg.

Bory whined louder as Clay started to heave the lifeless body to his shoulders and stagger with him up toward the ridge. He slipped a couple of times, but regained his footing just in time.

"Stop carrying on, Bory. He's just a runaway, but the Good Book says we can't let no critter die if we can help it."

Inside the cabin at last, Clay eased the dead weight from his shoulders onto a mattress ticking in one corner. The boy did not stir. Clay unfastened the sword from the boy's rope belt and laid it on the table.

18

He tried to remember what Pa had taught about frostbite. The boy's thin-soled shoes were wrapped all around and padded up and down both legs with blanket strips and pieces of knotted string. He unwound the blanket strips, put them over the back of a kitchen chair to dry, and pulled off the shoes.

He went outside and scooped up a gourd of snow.

Grabbing a fistful of it, he took a deep breath, and rubbed some on the boy's feet, hands, and face. He was careful not to rub where the trap marks showed. The boy's eyes fluttered, but that was all. Clay then rubbed the boy's feet with sorghum molasses and soda, feeling a strange mixture of distaste, yet a stubborn pride in doing a job well.

Clay looked at the places on the boy's legs where the trap had left its teeth marks. They weren't too deep, thanks to the padding of blanket strips the boy had tied about his legs. But there were little holes, and blood oozed up now through them.

Clay felt a twinge, thinking that if it had been Pa's big bear trap, the leg would have been broken, smashed for sure. He brought up some coal oil from the cellar and with a small rag he dabbed some on the marks. When the boy stirred only a little, he turned up the jug and poured a lot of the healing fluid over the leg.

Then he went up into the loft, brought down every extra blanket he could find, and covered the boy.

This done, he laid more logs on the fire and built it up to a gradual brilliance. Soon the light touched every corner of the cabin with red and yellow and dancing gold.

The boy lay quite still.

"Keep an eye on him, Beauregard," Clay cautioned. He took the boy's sword from the table and hid it in the cupboard.

"Now," he said softly, "I'll skin us that rabbit."

Clay worked quickly over their catch, peeling the skin back as Clem and his Pa had taught him. All the while, he flung worried looks to where the boy lay. His rifle stood reassuringly nearby. Finally he tossed the rabbit skin aside for later stretching and drying, then threw the innards onto the porch for Beauregard.

He cut the rabbit flesh into small pieces and placed them in the pot to brown with a good-sized piece of the pork. When he heard it sizzle, he sighed and let Bory back inside.

Reaching for a string of the shucky beans left soaking overnight, he said to Bory, softly, "Lordy, but I'd give my right arm for an old dried-up onion!"

When the stew bubbled, Clay sat on a low stool to watch for motions from the boy. He wondered if he had done everything proper. Pa always cautioned that the worst part for frostbite were the fingers and toes and the ears and nose.

After a while the sun pushed through the cracks around the door and Clay knew it would be warming up a little outside. He went out and undid the wood shutters and shoved them back, letting in some sun and fresh air.

About noon, the boy stirred.

He moved his head to one side. Clay stiffened. He stood up and watched the boy as he fluttered his eyelids, trying to open them.

"Don't fret," Clay cautioned as softly as he knew how. "You'll be all right."

The boy's eyes sprang open at the sound of Clay's voice. The eyes were big and they held fear.

Clay took a step backward toward his gun. "You've been hurt," said Clay evenly. "Just lay back and I'll fetch you some dry clothes."

The boy's face seemed at once all eyes, the whites rosy in the fire glow as he watched Clay move to a nail and take

20

down some old clothing. When Clay threw him the clothes, he did not move to take them.

"Go ahead," said Clay. "I'll get you some juice from that stew over there while you change into those."

Clay went to the fireplace and ladled up some of the rich, brown juice from the bubbling pot. He did not hear the boy move to put on the clothes, so he shrugged and said, "Well, if you want to keep on them wet things—it's all right by me."

Clay set the bowl on the table, then turned to rearrange the things drying in front of the fire. He took his time about it, because he heard the boy stirring and figured he was changing his clothes.

"Just throw me the wet ones," he said, "and I'll put 'em with these others."

Finally, Clay turned and the boy was standing, shakily, before him. Clay's old blue homespun shirt hung on the boy's frame like a loose extra skin. The boy tried to take a step toward the table, but he stumbled forward, grabbing the back of a chair to keep upright.

"You ain't got the strength of a flea yet," said Clay. "Get back over there and I'll fetch you the broth."

The boy returned to his pallet and took the bowl then, his eyes never for a moment leaving Clay's face. He looked to the dog standing silently beside Clay. Finally he turned up the bowl and drank from it, his hands trembling.

"Easy," cautioned Clay.

After draining the bowl the boy flung a look of gratitude to Clay and a weak smile played on his lips. His teeth were white and strong.

Sinking back onto his pallet, filled with corn shucks that rustled, the boy sighed deeply and soon was asleep again.

In the early afternoon, when Clay decided the stew was

cooked, he served himself a helping, gave some to Bory, and saved some for the boy. He left the cabin several times after he decided the boy was too puny to do him any harm. He and Bory finished checking the line, but found nothing except a skinny chipmunk.

He took some fire logs from the shed to the small porch, and placing them on a block, chopped them into kindling. He took Lazy Girl to the spring for water. In some places where drifts were high, she had to plow through with effort, the snow leaving white frosting beneath her belly. Clay broke a thin skim of ice for her to drink.

As the cold sun started to dip into the west, and the boy still seemed to sleep soundly, Clay took Bory tracking. He got off a shot at a deer, but missed.

They tracked the deer a while until, fretful about the boy, Clay whistled for Bory to turn back.

When the sun had melted into the horizon and the mists could no longer be seen about the ridges, Clay wondered if something was bad wrong with the boy. Remembering the dread fever of last fall, he tiptoed to where the boy lay and touched his forehead with the tip of his finger.

The skin was dry and cool.

Clay shrugged and said to Bory, "I guess he's all right. Just tuckered out." He went to the table and lighted the lamp, then went outside to bolt the shutters tight. "Well, let him sleep. I got me some whittling to do."

After eating some corn pone, soaked in the juice from the stew, Clay brought out a wood carving, a half-finished bird. A towhee in flight.

The carving was of soft pine, and Clay ran his fingers over the nice grain. He was shaping the bird so the dark knot would be where the eye of the bird was supposed to be. The other two knots, streaks really, looked like brown shadows on the outstretched wings.

Clay held the bird to the lamp and admired it. It was right pretty. He was proud of it.

He figured, too, he could think best while whittling. There was something about using his hands that turned his mind free to ramble.

The boy's presence in the cabin made him uneasy. Clay didn't like his being there. But at least Clay had done his Christian duty and kept him from freezing. When the boy awoke again, he'd rub more coal oil over those places on his leg. He'd feed him, and as soon as he was strong enough, he'd send him on his way.

Wasn't more a body could do.

He wondered where the boy had come from, where he was going. It seemed peculiar, his being here in this part of the mountains by himself.

Clay stopped whittling. A dark suspicion. He remembered warnings about strangers.

He got up, quickly, and went to the cupboard. Opened it quietly . . . quietly. Then he relaxed. The fancy sword was still hidden there.

3

IT WAS STILL DARK when Clay awoke. He had slept all night in his clothes, fitfully, beside his rifle, getting up several times to keep the fire built up. It had been a long time since anyone had stayed in the cabin with him—except Beauregard—and Clay was alert to the slightest rustling whenever the boy moved in his sleep. Even his breathing seemed uncommonly loud there in the cabin where no other sound was heard except the wind and Bory's thump-thump on the floor when he scratched.

Clay tiptoed quietly to the cupboard and took out the sword. He carried it to the fireplace and looked at it. It was the prettiest thing he had ever held in his hands. It had silver on the top and fancy letters on the scabbard. Clay traced the fancy letters with his finger. They were finely drawn, like a spider's webbing, and the handle fit his hand like a worn glove.

He pulled the sword from its scabbard. Striking a pose, he tested it against an imaginary enemy and was pleased at his bold black shadow on the far wall. In a moment, he was fighting at Petersburg. He was fighting off a grim-faced Yankee, coming at him with blood in his eye, his blue hat askew . . . then another, a Yankee sergeant twice his

24

size. Easily he finished them off and looked for other adversaries.

Presently he bumped into a chair and the boy awoke. Embarrassed, Clay slid the sword quickly into its scabbard and laid it on the table.

"You awake?" he said. "You all right?"

The boy did not move or answer.

Reading the boy's feelings, Clay spoke again in a calm, quiet voice. "I'm Clay Gatlin. I hauled you outta one of my traps yesterday morning. Ain't nobody gonna hurt you."

The boy looked around. He opened his mouth to speak but closed it again. Clay began to wonder if the boy could talk.

"What you doin' up here?" asked Clay. "You lost?"

The boy still did not answer, and Clay wanted to shake him.

He wanted to shake him and make him talk and, somehow, make him feel sorry for causing all the trouble about the war. In this feeling was mixed up his grief about Pa being killed . . . and all the rest.

Another instinct, a feeling he couldn't pin down, told him this boy could spell trouble. That sword—he'd probably stolen it. He probably would lie and cheat and cause no end of trouble.

"Can't you talk?"

The boy, seeming to sense the hostility in Clay's tone, turned back the blankets and leaned on one shaky elbow. His smile riled up a nameless anger in Clay when he said, "You can look at that sword some more if you want."

Clay shrugged and placed a log on the fire, then stirred it to new life with the poker. "It don't interest me that much," he lied. He swung the pot over the highest flame. "I'll heat you up some of this stew. You look like you could use some."

The boy didn't bother to say thank you, and this riled Clay more than the smirking smile.

"Where am I?" the boy asked, his eyes darting cautiously around the cabin. "Did you bring me here?" He continued to look around the cabin.

Knowing what the boy's thoughts were, Clay said, "You can go outside if you want. Out behind that big tree."

When the boy came back in, walking feebly, he asked about the rest of Clay's family.

"My folks are gone," said Clay quickly. "They—uh— they'll be back."

Fear returned to the boy's eyes, and Clay felt no strong urge to ease the boy's mind. But he said, in spite of himself, "Nobody's gonna harm you. Here—if you'll get to the table, this stew will fill your empty spots."

While Clay dished up stew into a tin plate, the boy limped to the table and sat down. Clay placed the plate in front of him.

"How'd you get way up here in the mountains?" asked Clay, studying the boy's face. "You by yourself?"

The boy nodded and started to eat the food before him. Between mouthfuls he said, importantly, "I'm on my way to Washington City!"

Clay felt a stab of excitement.

"But how'd you get—"

"This farmer man," said the boy, "he was goin' along the road in this wagon and I was tired—so I hopped in." He tried to laugh, but it came out more of a mouth-filled grunt. "I pretty soon fell asleep, and when I opened my eyes, that wagon she was settin' in the middle of noplace up in the mountains. Near here, I guess. I gets out and starts walking. When it starts snowing so hard, I don't know which way to go." He looked around again. "Where is this place?"

26

"Sevier County," said Clay.

"We still in Tennessee?"

Clay nodded. He unconsciously fingered the sword on the table and the boy took quick notice.

"Took that off a Union cal-vary soldier," he said. "He was laying in this little ditch. He had his mouth open and his eyes was . . ."

"Didn't it make you scairt?" asked Clay, shivering. "Taking that off him? Maybe he was a general."

The boy finished the stew and licked his lips. "From the likes of that sword, I reckon he was." Then he grinned, showing a space where a tooth should be. "But gen'rl or no gen'rl, they don't use swords up in heaven . . . and if he be goin' to that other place—well, I figure all that terrible heat'd melt it right down!"

Clay smiled in spite of himself and started to relax a little. Yes, the boy could talk all right.

"Maybe he'll come back to haunt you."

"Maybe," said the boy thoughtfully, "but if I moves fast enough, he won't know where I is."

"How old are you?" asked Clay.

"Twelve, goin' on thirteen," he answered.

"A mite scrawny for twelve," muttered Clay, getting up to tend the fire. "How you figure on getting all the way to Washington?" He put the poker back in its place and studied the orange flame. Without turning around he added, "It must be hundreds and hundreds of miles from here."

He's plumb addled, Clay thought to himself. He'd have to walk through woods, and there'd be wildcats and maybe a bear riled from his sleep. There'd be hunger and bone-biting cold and sleeping on the wet ground . . . rain . . . freezing winds. Only the good Lord knew what dangers and hardships . . .

"I find a way," said the boy proudly.

Clay grudgingly admired his spunk. But he only scowled and asked, "But *why?*"

The boy came over to the fire and stared into it a long while. When he spoke, his voice was soft and Clay could hardly hear him over the crackle of the logs. "I aims to be where Mr. Lincoln is," the boy said.

Where Mr. Lincoln is. The words of his neighbor, John Brewster, came back to Clay. Brewster had said that all slaves thought the Yankee president freed them personal. The boy apparently thought this too.

"My Granny," said the boy in a whisper, "she wanted to go to Washington City. We was going together. We belong to this big plantation a few miles from Knoxville, me and my Granny—but . . ."

Just for the fleeting space of a heartbeat—or a sigh—Clay felt something for the boy. A kinship. The beginning, perhaps, of an understanding. But then, in the next moment, the old bitterness rose inside him. It beat in his temples and coursed through his veins and he demanded, "You a runaway?"

No answer from the boy.

Clay knew from John Brewster that some slaves were still held in Tennessee—that Tennessee was not among the states farther south that were named in the Emancipation Proclamation. But he also knew that Tennessee was the last state to leave the Union and would probably be the first to join the Union again when the fighting was over.

His Pa, who was quick to trade his plow for a gun to fight on the side of the Rebs, was still not all the way for "secesh." And most of his neighbors in the hills were downright against leaving the Union.

Clay started to ask the question again, but decided to let

it go. The boy, not answering, probably was a runaway. Probably lied, too, about how he got the sword. Probably took it off his master.

But so many slaves were leaving the plantations, one runaway among many would not be noticed.

As John Brewster said, few masters bothered these days to run after their slaves to bring them back. He said one grain of wheat in a whole wheat field didn't cause much notice.

"What they call you?" Clay asked.

"Mostly they call me Foxy," he said, "but my Granny, she called me Dan'l—like Dan'l in that lions' den. She said I'm like Dan'l," he declared. "She said I wasn't scairt of nothing."

"I know my Bible," snapped Clay.

Presently a bumping noise shook the door and Foxy jumped up, his eyes wild.

"Hide me! They've come to fetch me!"

Clay at once felt satisfyingly superior to the boy. He laughed. "Where you want me to hide you—up in the loft?"

"Anyplace," begged the boy in a whisper, "but don't let them take me!"

"Aw, stop fretting," said Clay in a disgusted voice. "That ain't nobody at the door. Lazy Girl—she's my mule. She sometimes works the catch loose on the shed."

The boy looked doubtful.

"Here, I'll show you." Clay opened the door and Lazy Girl stood there on the porch, her ears up, her head cocked sideways.

"You no-good mule!" yelled Clay. "I'm gonna trade you for a horse! Get back to that shed and I'll feed you proper!"

After Clay and the boy led the mule back to the shed and threw her some hay, they returned to the cabin.

Clay breakfasted on corn pone and turnips from the cold cellar, then fed Beauregard. Afterward, they went out to check the trap line.

Clay wasn't sure the boy would be able to go, limping like he was, but Foxy said he wanted to go with him. And Clay decided it would be better than having him alone in the cabin, butting his nose into things that wasn't his.

As they walked along, the snow squeaked under their feet, and Clay explained—in short grunts—where each trap lay and showed the boy how they worked. He told him what animals lived in the mountains. The boy asked a lot of questions and Clay gradually grew tired of answering. "Don't you know *nothing?*" he asked at last.

The boy looked hurt. "Course, I know *lots* of things. I ain't never been trapping, maybe, but I bet I know lots of things *you* don't know!"

Clay's look challenged him. "Like what?"

"Well," said Foxy smugly, "I can read and write! My master, he let me learn with his children. And I can mend clothes so you can't hardly tell it, and I can cook and I can make up songs too!"

Besides being a liar, thought Clay, he's boastful too. There wasn't hardly any sin worse than that. Still, he felt uncomfortable. He had never got around to learning his letters, but he couldn't let the boy know that.

"I can do all that," said Clay, " 'cept maybe make up songs. And I bet I could do that too, if I wanted."

They continued in silence, their feet making prints in the new snow. Finally, Clay said, "Bet you can't either make up songs. I dare you!"

"What kind of song you want?"

Clay looked around. It had to be something hard. A real test. "How 'bout a song about Old Bory, there? He's named for General Beauregard that's up in Petersburg right now. Bet you can't make up a song about him!"

The boy studied the dog a minute, wrinkled his brow. Then he smiled.

"Beauregard . . . Ole Beauregard . . . he's as big as a tub of lard . . ." he sang in a high-pitched, but musical voice. "Thought he was a ladies' dan . . . then Gen'rl Lee picked another man!"

Clay, impressed but cautious, shrugged. "I guess you can make up songs, all right."

"Sure," said Foxy. "I can make up songs about anything."

Back home that afternoon with a catch of two rabbits and a squirrel, the boys warmed themselves by the fire, and Clay asked, "I been studying it out. I think maybe I better guide you down out of this mountain."

Foxy looked surprised.

"You'd just get lost again." The boy did not answer and Clay asked, "When you think you'll feel like gettin' on?"

Foxy considered. "Tomorrow, maybe . . . or the next. I gotta be getting on to Washington City."

"Think you can travel on that leg?"

"Sure. It feels right fine now."

Clay studied the fire. "Mighty long way . . . Washington."

"Yeah," said Foxy. "If I just had me a horse or a mule and some supplies . . ."

Clay stiffened and said angrily, "Well, don't go thinking you can steal mine!"

Foxy smiled. "I ain't thinkin' of stealin' her. How'd you like to trade that no-good animal for this fine sword?"

Clay snorted. But then he studied the sword and wondered if maybe he just couldn't get him another plowing

31

mule come spring. The sword would be a mighty fine thing to own.

"No," he said at last. "I couldn't get along without my mule. Besides, my Pa left her to me."

Foxy's eyes widened. "Your Pa! I thought you said—"

Clay turned his head away angrily. "Never mind what I *said*. My Pa's dead . . . killed in the war . . ."

"And your Ma?"

"Fever took her. Last fall."

The boy started to say he was sorry, but Clay cut him short. "And I don't want no pity!"

Foxy was silent for a while. Then he asked matter-of-factly, "Ain't you got no folks?"

Clay nodded. "Got a brother. He's in Washington City."

Foxy looked quickly to Clay's butternut coat, hanging on a nail. "A Reb! In Washington City?"

Clay nodded. "He joined up with the Feds before the war commenced. Pa wouldn't let us speak his name after that." Clay turned from the fire to begin supper. He sliced a thin piece of the salt pork and started to skin the rabbit.

He made no protest when the boy came over and began to help him cut the meat into small pieces. He noticed from the corner of his eyes that the boy handled a knife well. Finally he admitted to himself the boy at least spoke the truth when he said he could cook.

Clay got out his whittling while the stew simmered, and Foxy threw the innards onto the porch for Beauregard. "Damn him!" said Clay under his breath, though he was not accustomed to using strong language. "Been here since yesterday morning and he's starting to act like he owns the place!"

Clay worked in angry silence, wondering if the boy was planning to steal his dog too when he left.

Finally, in a mellower mood, Clay said, "Sure would be

fine to see Clem again. Him and me's the only Gatlins left."
He let his finger slide along the smooth surface of the pine
bird. "I think I'll fairly bust sometimes to see him."

Foxy studied Clay's face a while before he asked cautiously, "Why don't you go to Washington City too? We'd
have us a fine time. Why, you could see places you ain't
never seen, and we could do chores for folks and make
money, and we could take Ole Bory—"

"And the mule," snapped Clay.

Foxy scratched his head. "Well, sure, the mule would be
a mighty fine help."

Clay studied the fire again, spluttering and spitting. "See
the spittin' fire?" he asked. "That means it's gonna come a
fresh snow tonight. If it gets any deeper, Lazy Girl wouldn't
get through the drifts."

"It might not," said Foxy.

Clay stopped whittling and considered the idea. It was a
big idea, bigger than any he had held inside his mind before
. . . and he had to turn it over carefully.

Washington City.

Clem.

He did not fight the pain and longing that filled him suddenly.

It was almost fateful the way the boy had come. And he
talked about the very thing that had been playing in a secret
corner of Clay's mind for such a spell.

He was all alone now. Nobody left to guide him—to help
him walk in the right way. Except Clem.

"No, it'd be plumb crazy," said Clay, resuming his whittling. "The snow's too deep, and we'd probably starve. Besides, I belong here. This is my home."

Foxy, seeming to sense hesitation in Clay's voice, rushed
to take advantage. "Mister Clay, you could see some fine
sights. Why, I hear in Washington they's jobs for everybody

33

and you can make more money than you can shake a stick at. You could come back here when you wearied of travelin', and you'd be so rich you could buy yourself a new plow, and maybe some pigs too. They're mighty fine eatin'!"

Clay thought of his Pa. How would Pa feel if he went up there and mixed with Yankees? They were different from Southern folk. He thought, too, of the mountains in the spring. He'd always been there when the first crocus pushed up through the snow, and he'd always watched the robins skittering around the trees, building their nests, and the wild honey bees weaving their black nets around the flowering dogwood.

But hadn't he always hankered to see the rest of the country that lay behind the mist-covered mountains? Hadn't he always promised himself the sights of such? A sense of adventure stirred and quickened his senses.

Washington was surely a long ways off. But he was wise in the ways of the woods and streams, and they could always trap and fish when they got hungry. He remembered John Brewster telling about a railroad, the East Tennessee and Virginia, that ran all the way from Knoxville to Charlettsville in Virginia. He believed they could make it to Knoxville. Then, if they followed those tracks, it couldn't be far from Charlettsville to Washington City. Of course, he didn't hanker to travel with the boy, and he'd likely have to watch him sharp.

Still, the boy did know how to read and write and he could cook—maybe he could be useful in other ways. If only they could get Lazy Girl through the drifts, he knew in his bones they could make it.

"No, I can't go," he said, "but I'll pack you some vittles in the morning if your leg's all right. And I'll guide you down off this mountain."

4

IN THE MOONLIGHT just before morning the little crosses behind the cabin were pale silver-gray. Clay stood looking down at them a long time.

He had heard the gentle drip of the melting snow when he awoke suddenly after a vivid dream. In his dream of the night, Clem had spoken to him and reached out his arms. And Clay took this for a sign. When he came fully awake, feeling as though some unseen hand had shaken him, he heard what was to him another sign—the melting of the snow. An unexpected break in the weather.

He had dressed quickly and slipped outside in the darkness.

He stood there on the sodden ground, his tall dark-clothed figure covered in misty light, and turned over in his mind what he should do. The weather was, miraculously, breaking. There was a mild breeze that ruffled the black hemlock branches and sent little skiffs of snow blowing down the mountain from the ridge. But most of the snow was melting. Already, in spots where there were no drifts, there were huge patches of brown earth, black now in the pale light.

They would be able to get through the hills to lower land.

Clay knew now he would go with the boy to Washington City.

He sighed, letting his soul fill with the pain of leaving, yet with the sweet anticipation of seeing his brother again. "Pa," he said quietly to the small wooden cross at his feet, "is things always so hard?" Life had been so easy with his Ma and Pa always telling him what was best. Now he was alone and had to decide things for himself. It would take a lot of getting used to. If only he could be with Clem again. Clem could help him decide things.

He bent and plucked a wet leaf from the smooth grave of his Pa, and his hand lingered for a moment on the cross. He gently ran his finger over the wood, then let his hand rest on the other two, Ma's and little Davey's.

"I'll be back soon," he promised fiercely. "I'll try to bring Clem back with me. And I'll be a true Rebel, like you, Pa. You'll never be ashamed of me—I'll promise you that! And that slave boy—don't you worry 'bout me falling into beggar trash 'cause of him. Only reason we're going together"—he looked around for the right word—"is 'cause he's just a convenience. That's all."

He heaved a sigh and hurried back to the cabin.

When the boy awoke, rubbing his eyes, the sun was up and Clay already had waterproofed matches by dipping them into hot candle wax, lined up all available foodstuffs and cooking utensils, and folded extra blankets neatly on the table. A leather pouch at his waist held dried moss for fire tinder, as well as a piece of flint and steel. A sheath at his waist held his hunting knife. Fishing hooks were carefully tucked inside a brown felt hat that he would wear.

"I don't need all *them* things," said the boy, surprised.

"I'm going to Washington City," Clay said.

The boy's eyes told Clay he was pleased, but Clay's stern look made him hold back his expression of joy. The boy

36

dressed quickly and joined Clay with preparations for their journey.

In exactly two hours they had eaten breakfast, fed and watered the mule, fed Beauregard, boarded up the windows with cut nails, loaded their meager food supplies and utensils onto Lazy Girl's back. Small panniers, found inside the shed, served to hold the food, while the top pack held extra clothing, bedding, Clay's wood carving, two small traps, an ax, a rope, grain for the mule, some beaver furs, and a worn piece of canvas. Clay carried his flintlock with extra shot and powder over his shoulder. Extra clothing and a ball of string filled Foxy's haversack.

Clay patted Lazy Girl's flanks and spoke gentle to her, hoping all the while her stubbornness wouldn't make her balk at the heavy pack. He sweet-talked her and gave her a little extra grain, with a turnip for a treat.

Giving a final look around the cabin, Clay said, "I reckon it's as tight as can be. Guess I oughta leave John Brewster a note, 'cause he might come here 'fore he decides to make his next trip down to Findlay's." He looked quickly to his hand. "I—uh—pinched my hand this morning in one of the traps . . . uh—maybe you could—"

"Sure," said Foxy amiably, "I'll write the note for you."

Clay wondered if the boy suspected the truth . . . that he could not write. But at least Foxy didn't let on.

Clay explained what the boy was to say. Then he took the note from him and placed it in the center of the table, where Brewster could find it. He had the boy add to the note, then, that he would be obliged if Brewster would board up the door after himself.

After Clay bolted the door, he placed the chopping block in front of it to hold against the wind and rain.

"Well," said Clay with confidence he didn't feel, "let's be gettin' on."

It was right, his going to Washington City to see Clem. It's what he had to do. Yet . . .

Looking back for that last moment, before leading Lazy Girl down the little dip beyond the big tulip tree that would cut off his sight of the cabin—maybe forever—Clay stopped.

His heart pounded and his mouth went dry.

For a thin Yankee dime he'd go back, unload the pack, and tell the boy to go on without him. He closed his eyes tight, just for the space of four heartbeats, trying in that moment to remember every single thing about the cabin— the tomahawk dent beside the chimney, the gently sloping roof where the sun now glistened, the little window light now covered with crude planks, the front porch where Ma used to sit and snap beans . . .

For a while the world stood still.

"You coming?" asked Foxy impatiently.

Clay opened his eyes and forced them to look forward to the trail. "Yeah," he said fiercely, trying to hold back the tears that burned beneath his eyelids, "I'm comin'!"

All morning the boys made their way down the steep, twisting, rock-jagged mountain trail, Clay leading Lazy Girl, Bory running alongside, Foxy bringing up the rear, his sword at his waist. The trail was crisscrossed in places by little rivulets of melting snow, and at times Lazy Girl had to be coaxed to continue. The sun warmed them some, but the breeze made them turn up the collars of their coats.

Clay wore his floppy hat, his heavy brown jacket, tied with frayed cord, and Foxy wore his red woolly cap, one of Pa's coats, and Pete's old boots. The boots were big and they had stuffed rags in the toes to make them fit.

The boy seemed nimble-footed considering his hurt leg, but he chattered so much that Clay finally had to shut out the steady stream of words by concentrating on other matters. At last, when he could shut out the chatter no longer, he called back, "Better put your mind to what you're doing. It's a long way to the bottom of this mountain, and they's some mean turns."

The boy walked in silence for a while after that. Then he started in to sing. "Beauregard . . . Ole Beauregard . . . he's as big as a tub of—"

At one bad turn, where the mountain dropped off sharply, he stumbled and started to roll.

"Watch it!" shouted Clay. "Roll into that gully—it'll stop you!"

The boy rolled about ten to fifteen yards down the mountainside before landing in a little dip filled with melting snow. He looked up at Clay and grinned. "Them boots . . ."

Clay snorted. "Wasn't them boots! If you'da paid a mind to what you was doing. Well, don't just *lay* there! Get up here 'fore you're soaked clean through!"

Clay sighed. Now they'd have to build a fire. He hadn't planned to build a fire yet. But now they would have to.

Back on the trail, Foxy asked, "How we gonna find dry wood?"

Clay, again feeling superior to the boy, grunted, "Easy. They's always plenty of rotten wood laying under thick branches and such. I'll show you." Clay tied Lazy Girl's lead rope to a tree and stomped off into the underbrush, Beauregard and Foxy at his heels.

Clay stopped, finally, beside a fallen tree that still held small branches. "Start breaking off these," he said. "No, not there—down underneath, where it's dry."

The boy did as he was told.

Soon they had a number of branches and Clay also had some good dry pieces of birchbark and some scraps of the dry, oily insides of the dead tree.

He pointed to the green hemlock, so thick and green they could hardly see the sky through it. "See those green branches?" he asked. "These are what we can break off at night when we need a lean-to."

"What would we lean the branches to?" asked the boy.

Clay pointed to a piece of upright deadwood, bent in two, making a triangle. "Something like that. See, you pick the growing branches and prop them in layers against that upright stuff. Be sure it's sturdy first. It keeps out the wind."

They walked back to where Lazy Girl was tied.

"But we won't make no lean-to tonight," said Clay. "We gonna sleep in Mr. Findlay's barn, where we can get hay for Lazy Girl."

"Who's Mr. Findlay?" asked Foxy.

"He runs that store I told you about—the one at the foot of this mountain. I trade with him for flour and such. Take furs to him for tradin'."

"Will he let us use his barn?"

"Sure. Mr. Findlay's all right."

"Why don't we just sleep in the woods," asked Foxy, "and feed Lazy Girl some of that grain we brought along?"

"We save that till we need it," explained Clay. "Long as we travel near farms, we try to exchange chore work for hay. When we can't find no farm, then we *have* to feed her the grain."

Tired of explaining, Clay busied himself with the fire.

First he took the birchbark scraps and placed them, with some of the oily chips of dead wood, into a little heap. Above this he placed, wigwam fashion, pine stubs and cones found lying in protected areas. He built the little wig-wam, using the other small wood pieces they had collected.

Then he lighted one of the waterproof matches by strik-ing it on a rock.

The dead wood and birchbark ignited quickly, and presently he unsheathed his knife and made little wood shavings, which he fed to the first feeble flames. Some of the bigger wood pieces started to catch, and soon the fire was crackling.

Foxy stripped off his outer clothes and lined them up over a stick in front of the fire. While he was roasting in his long underwear and the clothes were drying, Clay put some sassafras bark into a pot of water and boiled it until it was a deep, rich color. He fried a hoecake of cornbread, which he shared with Foxy and Beauregard, and the two boys drank their tea slowly, letting it warm their stomachs.

Finally, when Foxy's clothing was dry, he dressed quickly. Clay put out the fire and untied Lazy Girl. Leading her once more down the mountain trail, he said a silent, urgent prayer that the boy wouldn't take another tumble before they reached Findlay's.

It was dusk when they arrived, tired and hungry. Mr. Findlay, a huge man with a barrel-shaped stomach and a friendly red face, greeted Clay. "Where you been, Clay? Haven't seen you for a spell!"

Clay returned the warm greeting and asked, "Can I get some supplies for these?" He flung the beaver skins over the counter.

"Sure," said Mr. Findlay, feeling the texture of the skins and running the heel of his hand along the pelts.

"I'm going to Washington City," said Clay.

A pair of keen blue eyes looked up quickly. "You goin' to see Clem?"

Clay nodded.

Findlay rubbed his chin. "Mighty long way to be traveling."

"I know."

"How you figurin' on going?"

"Thought we'd walk along the railroad as far as Charlettsville," said Clay.

"We?"

Clay nodded toward Foxy, who was warming himself by the potbellied stove in the rear of the store. "He got himself lost up on my ridge . . . was on his way to Washington City." Clay shrugged. "Thought I'd go along."

Findlay laughed. "Now, Clay, I know you ain't decided to go just as easy as that! Must have give a heap of thought."

Clay nodded. "I did."

"Do you have plenty of supplies, boy? Stuff for fires? An ax?"

Clay nodded to all of these. "I could use some beans and some salt pork, if you have any. Few onions maybe. Little powder. And some hard cash."

Findlay laughed again. "That ain't easy to come by, but I'll see what I can do." He leaned over the counter, then, and said in a whisper. "That boy—can you trust him?"

"I suppose."

"Lots of folks might make it hard on you—with him along."

"I promised," said Clay flatly.

"Well, just wanted you to know what you might be up against." Findlay scratched his head and looked thoughtful. "I don't know . . . mighty long way to Washington. Though it does seem smart to follow the rails if you can . . . and to have somebody along if they'd be of help. Tell you what, though, better watch out for patrols. Last fall the railroad was in Yankee hands, but now the Rebs have it again. They're keeping patrols all along the line. They might not take kindly to anybody—"

"We'll look out," said Clay.

42

"Another thing," said Findlay, "the Rebs is conscripting fourteen-year-olds. How many years are you, Clay?"

"Be fourteen in June," said Clay.

"Got proof someplace?"

"It's in the family Bible."

Findlay scratched his head. "I don't know—you look tall for your age. They might grab you and swear you in. You got that Bible with you?"

Clay shook his head. "Just got me a small one here." He patted his shirt pocket.

"Well," said Findlay, "just you look out."

Clay wasn't sure he didn't want to be conscripted—if it wasn't for his promise to his Ma . . . and his wanting to see Clem so bad.

Clay felt a blast of air and turned to see a tall mountain woman entering the store. She wore a black hat pulled down to her ears, and her mouth was a hard, thin line. She came closer to the counter, saw Clay, then stared at him in a way that made him feel uncomfortable. Her eyes, hard blue stones, held unmistakable hatred, and she was directing that hatred straight at Clay!

Thinking she had mistaken him for someone else, Clay tried to smile, but the woman continued to stare. Before Clay knew what she was about, she spat, "Dirty Reb!"

"I—I—"

Ignoring Clay's red face, she turned to the store owner and said, in a shrill voice, " 'Pears like you serve any kind of beggar trash in this store!"

After the woman had purchased some salt pork and a piece of red flannel cloth, she went out, banging the door so hard the food tins rattled on the shelves.

Clay turned to the storekeeper. "Why did she say that? I don't reckon I even know her."

The storekeeper shook his head. "That's Mrs. Garroway.

She lost two boys in the fighting. They were Unionist upris-ers. She knew you, I guess, from havin' seen you with your Pa." He shook his head sadly. "And you air the spittin' image of him."

He fingered the beaver furs again, lowering his eyes quickly. "Guess she figures your Pa and those like him was to blame for the Unionist movement failing in Tennessee."

Clay felt his face grow hotter. "But it wasn't supported! It woulda failed anyway! That's what John Brewster—"

"I know," admitted the burly man, "but when folks is hurt . . . well, there ain't no reasoning." He looked at Clay again, this time his eyes filled with a plea for understand-ing.

Clay shivered. He had never been blamed before for something he had no hand in. It gave him a helpless feeling.

Later, in the barn where Lazy Girl had been fed and stalled for the night, Clay thought some more about what Mr. Findlay had said. He put his arms behind his head and stared at the darkness around him. Then, with one arm, he pulled Beauregard closer. He still felt the sting of the woman's words and glance. It was awful to feel such hatred.

Patting Bory's cold nose, Clay thought somehow that the woman's feelings were mixed up with the way he felt about the boy, but he was asleep before he could get it all straightened out in his mind.

5

"RUN, BOYS, RUN . . . the pat-er-ol ul catch you. Run, boys, run, you bet-ter get a-way. Char-ley run, Char-ley flew, Char-ley tore his shirt in two . . ."

Foxy was singing in his high-pitched voice as they tramped along toward Greeneville, where, Mr. Findlay had told them that morning, they could pick up the railroad, saving them a backtracking of nearly fifty, maybe sixty, miles into Knoxville. So Clay had abandoned his original plan to start the line just outside Knoxville and was cutting across the mountains, instead, in a northeast direction, to pick up the tracks at Greeneville.

"You make up that song?" asked Clay.

Foxy shook his head. "Was a song we used to sing."

"What does that mean—'the paterol 'ul catch you'?"

Foxy stared at the plank road they were walking, a mournful expression crossing his face. "They was mean men with guns and dogs. They looked out after dark. We couldn't go nowhere . . ." His voice cut off and all that could be heard was the clump-clump of Lazy Girl's hooves on the logs and the distant rush of water over a gorge.

Clay supposed the boy meant that slave owners, fearful

of an uprising, had their own patrols so their slaves couldn't go out after dark, but he didn't ask the boy any more.

"Well," said Clay thoughtfully, "when we start following that railroad we gotta look out for a different kind of patrol."

"You mean Yankees?"

"No—Reb patrols."

Foxy seemed surprised. "But you a Reb—they wouldn't bother you!"

Clay, remembering the woman back at Findlay's store, and thinking how most of the hill people were Unionist sympathizers, shook his head. "They might not believe me," he said. "Besides I don't think they want nobody walking along them tracks. They's all kinds of spies and such, pretending to be picture takers and cake sellers."

"And boys gettin' on to Washington City," laughed Foxy, apparently pleased that someone might take him and Clay for spies.

"Just the same," said Clay, "we can't take no chances. We'll have to keep a sharp eye."

They had been walking since the first pink of morning, following corduroy roads, narrow mountain passes, and bridges. The cold pinched their faces and a leaden sky threatened snow.

Clay's stomach rumbled with hunger and his feet throbbed, but he didn't want the boy to know that.

"Think we can make Greeneville by night?" asked Foxy.

"We better," said Clay glumly, " 'cause Lazy Girl, she ain't fixin' to be coaxed much farther."

The forest began to loom dark and cold beside them, and Clay's eyes sought signs of an approaching town.

Finally he smiled and pointed. "Look—up there! Up the road! We must be close to a town."

"That farm," said Foxy, "she looks mighty good!"

46

The farm, isolated on a rise, was surrounded by tall mountains. Smoke curled from the chimney. Clay told Foxy to hold the mule's rope while he and Bory went up to the house to ask for some hay and shelter for the night.

Leaving his flintlock with the boy, Clay started up the long, winding road. As Clay and Bory got near the house, a mustard-colored dog ran out and barked at them. Holding Bory back, Clay said to the strange dog in low tones, "It's all right, feller. We ain't gonna hurt nobody."

"Who's there?" a woman asked from a crack in the front door. "What do you want?"

Clay introduced himself and explained his need for hay for his mule and a shelter for the night. As he talked, he could see two small children—a boy who looked about eight and his little sister—come up behind their mother and clutch her skirts.

"If we could just use your barn, ma'am," he said, "we'd be no trouble, and we'd be pleased to do chores."

The woman opened the door a little wider and looked closely at Clay and his dog. She was almost pretty except for being too gaunt, and her hair was tied back with a string.

"Well," she said slowly, "I *could* use some firewood."

"We'd be obliged to chop it for you in the morning," said Clay.

"I need it tonight."

Clay's heart sank. They were tired and it would be a great effort. But he said, "Yes, ma'am. I'll just go get Foxy."

"One thing more," the woman called after him. "I don't trust strangers in my barn at night, but you can feed your mule all the hay it wants, then be on your way."

As they chopped wood, just behind the back porch of the house, the small boy came to empty a dishpan of water, and

47

he stopped to talk with them. He had tousled, sun-bleached hair topped with a Reb kepi hat, and he seemed older than Clay had at first guessed. He told Clay about the trouble they were having with their Pa off to war. He said that the "Gov'ment im-press-ment" of their produce had made them really poor. "And the cav'lry," said the boy, shaking his head, "they done took everything that was growing."

"You mean the Yankees?" asked Foxy.

The boy shook his head. "And the Rebs too. They both took what they wanted without askin'."

Clay could understand the Yankees doing such a thing, but for the Rebs to do this to their own people was unthinkable.

"One soldier came back," said the boy, "and give me this." He tapped his kepi hat proudly. "Like the one Pa wears!"

When the woman came outside again, she was carrying a musket, and she looked at Foxy with narrowed eyes. Turning to Clay, she said, "You can get on down to the barn now and feed that mule." She looked again at the pile of wood. "I reckon you did a right good job."

"Thank you."

"There's a heap of good treed places further down the road, past that little bridge. You won't have no trouble bedding down there. Greeneville's 'bout eight miles as the crow flies . . . little longer by the road."

"Thank you," Clay said again. "Ma'am . . ."

The woman looked at him with a guarded expression, and her grip tightened on her musket.

"The little feller was telling me . . . I'm sorry about . . . Maybe it'll be over soon . . ."

The woman relaxed her grip on the musket and laughed. It was a hard, cold laugh without warmth or merriment.

48

"Well, I reckon it don't matter much whether it is or ain't. If my man ain't home soon to plant crops, we'll all be starved to death."

Clay felt helpless to answer.

"If another army passes here, God only knows what I'm gonna do. My old man better be fixin' to desert the army soon, and that's a fact!"

It was all written there in the woman's face—the privation, the weariness, the utter hopelessness of things. It was a strange war, Clay thought as they fed Lazy Girl and then started down the road for a place to sleep. A strange war where the home folk feared armies from both sides, and a man had to become a deserter to keep his family alive.

In about half an hour Clay had a roaring fire going and sassafras tea boiling in one pot and beans from Findlay's Store cooking in another with a slice of savory salt pork. He had left some of the salt pork with the little boy back there. Now he had half a notion to return to the farmhouse and offer some of their beans and other provisions. The woman and children looked so pitiful.

But it was dark and the woman might mistake them for foraging troops and blast them with that musket. It was too risky now. He should have thought of it sooner.

The beans smelled good and the sassafras was brewing. Some of the ash from the fire floated into the brew and blended with its rich orangy color.

Foxy looked to the starless sky and said, "Looks like a snowstorm coming."

"Yep."

"Reckon we got enough blankets and such?"

"This lean-to oughtta keep out most of it," said Clay confidently. "And being down in this little dip will help."

They were bedded down in a protected area, hemlock

and pine and cherry all around them. And the lean-to was sturdy, hardly letting a whisper of air through. Over the lean-to, Clay had thrown the canvas from their pack.

After eating, Clay directed Foxy to help take away the pothooks and poles. Next they drove a couple of stout poles into the ground behind the fire, slanting a little backward.

"Now," said Clay, "we'll pile up a wall of good stout logs, green or dry, against these. They'll throw the heat from the fire back into our lean-to."

"Want me to build up the fire?" asked Foxy.

Clay nodded. "Lay some smaller logs over it. We'll take turns keeping it built up during the night."

Presently, the reflecting wall was built and the fire roaring. Clay again checked Lazy Girl's position beneath a stand of hemlock, patted her comfortingly, and returned to his lean-to, where he stretched out and piled blankets over himself.

Beauregard burrowed beneath the blankets to lie on Clay's chest, Foxy fidgeted a while with his blankets, but finally all was quiet except for the crackling twigs on the fire and the rising wind singing a mournful song through the branches. The last thing Clay remembered was the hooting of a nearby owl and the thought that Clem would be mighty glad to see him if they ever reached Washington.

The insistent shrilling of a chickadee awoke Clay shortly after dawn. For a while he did not move. He just lay there beneath the warm blankets, sniffing in the fresh early-morning dampness of the air. He knew without looking that the fire would be almost out, so he got up, finally, and fed it some twigs and other dry tinder. He put on a pot of water for breakfast tea and looked around.

"Looky, Bory," Clay said to the dog, "look how white and pretty everything is." During the night the snow had

50

coated every bush and tree with a light, white frosting. Snow all around them had gathered itself into drifts and swirls, but in the little dip where their shelter was set the ground was free. The thick, green lean-to had kept out the wind and most of the snow. Branches above, heavy-laden, had protected them.

Clay looked to where Foxy slept. The boy was curled up in a ball, just the top of his red woolly cap showing.

Later, after breakfast, the boys loaded Lazy Girl's pack and set out for the town of Greeneville. They reached it well before noon.

It was a small, pretty town, situated in the foothills of the mountains. You could see the mountains, way off in the distance, gray, lighter gray, misty blue. The houses were huddled close together and many had little fences painted white. Some of the town folks were shoveling snow from the main street, and merchants were wiping their windows and sweeping footpaths.

Clay and Foxy walked down the middle of the street, looking neither left nor right. It was their plan to walk through the town, pass it, then backtrack through a wooded area and pick up the railroad at a point where there would be no picket station. At last they came to a livery stable where a group of men were gathered. Clay was glad they had thought to hide Foxy's sword in the pack under a blanket.

"Have you heard—the Feds have seized Charlestown!" one of the men was saying to the others. There was a murmuring and general outburst of opinions. Shortly, two gray-coated soldiers came down the street on horseback.

Clay looked after them and wished, just for that moment, that he could have shouted proudly, I'm a Johnny Reb too!

He was afraid of drawing attention, so he held back. Lots of folks probably had him figured for a mountain boy, and

51

with Foxy along maybe they would think he was a Union sympathizer. No use taking chances.

But at that farmhouse last night, he had thought of asking the little boy if he wanted to trade something for that Reb hat. He would be proud to wear it now.

They reached the railroad station, a small building with a red snow-covered roof. Except for a very old man sweeping the platform, it seemed deserted. Farther down the tracks they could see tents set up, and they figured this was patrol headquarters for that section of the line. Three soldiers were squatting around a fire, warming their hands and swapping stories.

"My but them tracks look purty!" exclaimed Foxy, grinning.

"You won't think so," snapped Clay, "if they lead us smack into a patrol!"

Going through the town, crossing the tracks, Foxy looked back and said, "And look at that little worn path along the grading for Lazy Girl!"

"That," said Clay, looking for a place to duck into the woods, "would be the trail for the horses of the patrols."

Behind some buildings they found a path leading into the woods. Circling back toward the railroad, keeping a sharp eye for soldiers, Foxy said, "You sure are fretful today, Mister Clay."

"Don't like patrols," said Clay.

Foxy furrowed his brow. "Neither do I. But we is here now . . . and them tracks is sayin', 'Come on, boys. I'll lead you where you want to go.' "

The sun broke free from the clouds and the tracks glittered. As the boys turned onto the small path that ran alongside the grading, Clay felt his spirits rise. His feet didn't hurt as much as they had the day before, and now

52

they had found the railroad, he felt, somehow, that they might just make it to Washington City.

He walked along, swinging his free arm in rhythm to his strides, and felt almost like joining in when Foxy started to sing.

"Run, boys, run, the pat-er-ol ul catch you. Run, boys, run, you bet-ter get a-way. Come on, Mister Clay, don't go borrowin' trouble!"

The sun burned on Clay's upturned face and brightened the ground all around them with an almost blinding radiance. Clay took a deep breath. By gum, he would join in. He was, suddenly, feeling that good.

Together, the two voices—Foxy's clear musical voice and Clay's deeper, not-quite-on-key voice—strangely blended.

"Char-ley run, Char-ley flew, Char-ley tore his shirt in two . . ."

6

THEIR FEET WERE SORE from walking, and their boots were wearing thin from the grating, grinding cinders. And, always, they were alert for pickets.

Clay felt pangs of homesickness as they traveled away from his beloved high mountains into valleys and foothills. He no longer felt protected, a part of mountain and forest and sky. The railroad's long iron arm led them through nameless towns with cold, friendless faces, twisted its way through hill passes and rocky crags, turned like a writhing snake along riverbanks, over bridges, beside the damp, quiet forest that always beckoned with its dark caverns. Walking along it, Clay felt, for the first time in his life, like someone he had become: a lanky, frightened hill boy who no longer fit into the scheme of things. A stranger to the land. An intruder.

"Ain't this fun?" Foxy would ask, balancing himself along the rails, placing one foot carefully in front of the other like a rope walker. "See," he exclaimed, "I can walk on these rails ten yards without fallin' off!"

And then they would hear the patrol in the distance, around some turn, and Clay, putting his finger to his lips, would quickly lead Lazy Girl off into the forest, or swamp marsh, or over some rocky ledges, until the patrol was past.

At night they slept in barns or in the woods in lean-tos, careful now to keep their fires low, letting only hot embers warm them through the nights. One morning they walked along, miserably, in a rainstorm until the downpour drenched them and cold water sloshed in their boots and they had to stop to build a fire to dry out.

While they were drying by the fire in their long underwear, they heard pickets close by. Quickly, they put out their fire and ran into the sheltering forest. Clay led Lazy Girl down into a little rocky gully, and his pulse pounded as he heard the soldiers stop not two hundred yards from them. Shivering from the cold rain and the wind, they had to lie on their bellies until the patrol moved away.

Several times they had trouble getting Lazy Girl over the railroad bridges. The first time Clay tried to coax her through the swift-moving narrow stream that ran about fifty feet below the bridge. She balked. Clay sweet-talked her, and Foxy tried singing to her and offering her treats. They both rubbed her neck and stroked her ears and told her what a good mule she was.

This failing, they tried force. Clay pulled on the lead rope and Foxy, his face sweating, pushed from behind. They couldn't get her to move a half inch.

At last Clay had an idea. He figured that if he would lead her to a spot farther downshore, where the stream was narrower and shallower, he could get way back and run with her. She always liked to run with him and Pa. He figured that when they reached the stream she would keep right on running and would leap over.

It was worth a try.

They walked downstream until they found a place where the stream was quite narrow, and little riffles could be seen making whitecaps over jutting rocks. "Here," said Clay, "this is a good place. We can jump over that easy—with a running start. I'll lead her back a ways, then start running."

Clay led Lazy Girl back into a farmer's meadow where snow still clung in patches beneath bushes and between rows of dead cornstalks.

When he decided they were back from the stream far enough, he clicked his tongue and, yanking on the rope, started to run. Lazy Girl immediately fell into the spirit of things and started to trot. Even with her pack, she ran as though she were having a fine frolic.

"Atta girl," encouraged Clay. "Let's keep going. Don't stop now," he said as he approached the narrow place. Lazy Girl kept running, and at the edge of the stream, Clay took a huge leap, still holding tight to the lead rope and yelling, "Jump—gal!"

Clay sailed in the air, still holding the rope, but Lazy Girl, abruptly becoming a mountain of resistance, stopped at the stream's edge. Clay landed midway in the stream, splashing water all around.

Foxy, standing on the opposite bank, laughed. "Oh— Mister Clay—if you ain't a sight!"

Soaked clean through, and cold, Clay looked at the stubborn animal. Lazy Girl looked back at him, her rope dangling at her feet. Her ears cocked impudently. It seemed to Clay she was asking, What are you doing in that cold water?

Getting to his feet, Clay said, "Well, gal, I guess you're smarter than both of us. I reckon we'll have to think up something else." He was humiliated, as well as chilled, but he tried to force a smile so that Foxy wouldn't sense his humiliation.

Foxy remembered seeing a deserted barn a ways back and the boys went back to the barn and took two long, wide planks. By laying the planks carefully over the ties in the railroad bridge, they gradually coaxed Lazy Girl across. When she would reach the end of the boards, Clay would coax her to stand carefully with feet planted firmly on the broad ties while Foxy slowly, carefully, moved the boards ahead. Looking down between the ties, Clay shuddered—if Lazy Girl should slip and fall . . .

His back ached and his fingers were still bleeding from having scraped them against sharp rocks in the stream below. And the wind made him shiver. When they finally made it across, he heaved a grateful sigh and hurried to find firewood.

On their sixth day of travel since Greeneville, their vittles were so low—all the salt pork gone and beans down to a handful—that Clay decided they would have to start trapping. They were now into a blustery, windy Virginia March and much of the snow had melted. But the wind still bit into them and chilled their bones.

They were beginning to get into the tall mountains again, and Clay felt a surge of joy when he saw his first spicebush and shrub yellowroot blooming near a stream. He felt a lump in his throat when he came across the first violets in the woodlands.

"Reckon we're gettin' into the Blue Ridge," said Clay with satisfaction. "See those mountains way off? They're almost as handsome as the Smokies."

Clay had heard that the land flattened out considerable after the Blue Ridge peaks. Somehow, he couldn't imagine a land without the tall, majestic peaks . . . blue haze clinging and the air so pure it made you feel achingly alive.

As they rounded a sharp turn, with towering rocks above them, Clay's sharp eyes caught sight of a great horned owl in a tall pine. It came to him that he could fell it with his rifle, but he threw the idea down, deciding that the noise of the shot would be too risky with patrols so active on this stretch of railroad.

"They might not hear it over the wind," said Foxy.

"No," Clay said, lowering his rifle. "Might be a patrol just around the next bend. We can't take that chance." After they continued on for a while, he said, "Tonight when we bed down, we'll set those traps. Maybe we'll fetch us a rabbit or a squirrel."

They asked at a farmhouse for hay and were told by a farmer that they could have hay for their animal, but were again refused shelter in the big barn.

Clay thanked the man and led Lazy Girl to the barn, where she ate as if she had not tasted hay for a month.

Before they left, the farmer told them to keep a sharp eye for pickets. " 'Pears to me," he said in his slow Virginia drawl, all the while eyeing Foxy with suspicion, "they's doing double duty on the line. Must be a troop train comin' through. Or maybe a hospital train, headin' for Knoxville."

Clay thanked him for his advice and started to leave.

"Another thing," drawled the farmer. "I hear tell they's mountain lions hereabouts. One, anyway. Ain't been much deer for 'em, and they be fierce hungry, I reckon. Hear tell two nights back one of 'em killed a cavalry mount."

As weary as he was, Clay's pulse quickened. In all the years he had lived in the mountains he had seen a mountain lion only once. His Pa had taught him that of all the mountain critters, the lion, or "painter," was the shyest, slyest, and most difficult to see. Clay knew that the big cat on his big soft feet could sneak away as quietly as a shadow. And he usually hunted his prey—generally deer—at night.

But one day when he and Clem had been hunting together, they had come upon one, sitting on a big rock about

58

one hundred yards away and partially hidden by brush. Clem cautioned Clay to be still, and they stood rooted to the spot. But before Clem could get his rifle sighted, a slight creak of a twig frightened the lion off. He had jumped gracefully from the rock and disappeared.

Clay heard that the mountain lion never attacked man, but, if hungry enough, would attack grown horses and even a bear. Of course, if you cornered one, he would likely claw you to bits without asking questions.

That night, snug beneath his blankets before the low fire, Clay heard a patrol. He stiffened and waited for the soldiers to pass.

"They sure is close," whispered Foxy. "Maybe we better stomp out our fire."

"Maybe—if we hear them again," said Clay.

After a little while Clay could no longer hear the men's voices, so he relaxed and started to drift off to sleep. The wind was quiet now and it was not so cold as it had been. Breathing deeply of the clean air, Clay decided spring would soon burst upon them.

Already he had seen the anglewing, the mourning cloak, and the little spring azure butterflies on the wing, and tiger beetles hurried before them in the woods. He hankered for home and the bursting of leaves from the mountain buds. If Washington City didn't seem so close now . . .

Clay must have slept, but something—a slight noise and a tensing of Beauregard—made him open his eyes. He whispered softly, "What is it, Bory?"

Foxy awakened too and asked, "What was that?"

"Don't know," said Clay. "Let's lay quiet and we'll find out."

Clay held Bory close and waited.

Finally, he heard a distinct rustling and Lazy Girl

59

stomped her feet restlessly and brayed. He flung a look to where she was tied and could make out her silhouette from the soft fire glow.

And then they saw him—the big cat, his silhouette barely discernible on a large rock above where Lazy Girl was tied. The lion, which Clay figured must be fully seven feet long from nose to tip of tail, was drawing his feet under him and hunching up his back.

Ready to pounce.

Clay knew the lion was swift and would leap to Lazy Girl's back, his deadly fangs sinking deep into her neck. He calculated, in a split second, what he should do. If he tried to get off a shot in the dim light, he might miss. Yet it might frighten the big cat away.

But the patrol might be close and the men might hear the shot in the still air.

Bory's hackles were up and he was growling deep in his throat. Clay knew that Bory would attack if he let him go and that the cat, instinctively fearing dogs, would probably be scared off. But maybe not before the damage had been done to Lazy Girl, standing now so helpless.

Just as the cat seemed to be gathering his rippling muscles into a springing position, Foxy acted. He leaped up from his bed and, grabbing his sword, charged the crouching animal. He flung the sword over his head as he ran, so the fire glow picked up the steel blade and made it glitter like a squirt of flame.

"Git! You lion, you!" shouted Foxy in his high, excited voice. "I'll run you through!"

The lion, frightened by all the noise and general commotion, retreated. He leaped from the rock and took off into the woods. Clay, who could hold Bory no longer, saw the dog streak off after the animal, yelping excitedly.

"Oh, Lordy," said Clay. "Now they'll hear us for sure."

Far off into the woods Bory ran, and Clay could hear his barking grow fainter and fainter.

"Quick!" said Clay. "Help me stomp out this fire. That patrol'll see it for sure now."

Just in time, the boys got the fire out and hovered quietly beneath hemlock branches. They could hear the soldiers tramping through the woods in the direction of Bory's barking. Clay prayed they wouldn't find him. Please, Bory, said Clay to himself. Don't let that cat fret you none. Come back. Please.

They lay huddled together for a long while. Presently, the men passed close to where they lay, waving lanterns and talking.

"Hear that?" asked one of the pickets. "Must be somebody out here with a dog!"

For a long time, Clay and Foxy trembled lest they be discovered. They listened while the soldiers thudded through the woods, then heard them give up and start back. Finally it was quiet again.

"Whew!" breathed Foxy. "That was a close one!"

Bory returned much later, panting hard. His tail was wagging excitedly.

"Got away from you, huh," laughed Clay. "Well, we don't need no mountain lion noways." He stroked the dog's coat and laughed. "Don't reckon I'd know how to fix up a mountain-lion stew."

Clay knew he should feel grateful to Foxy for his bravery. He had probably saved Lazy Girl from a bloody fate. Yet—he felt only a persistent resentment that now, because of the boy's foolhardy action, he was beholden to him.

The last thing Clay wanted was to feel beholden to anybody, especially to Foxy.

"You know," said Foxy, "I bet that big cat was at least five hundred pounds or more, and did you see them mean

61

eyes glowing in the dark? I tell you, my Granny, she'da been proud!"

There he goes, thought Clay bitterly, boasting again. That cat couldn'ta been over a hundred pounds, dressed.

"Yeah—I guess she woulda been proud," said Clay grudgingly. "Now, if you'll stop your jabbering, we'll get us some sleep."

Later, sleeping without building a new fire, the boys found it so cold and damp that they kept waking. Cramped and unable to move for the cold, Clay looked to where the boy slept and saw him shivering. Then he heard him crying in his sleep. Clay lay still, hoping for morning. Even if he wanted to, he was too rigid with cold himself to move and help Foxy's discomfort. Finally he nudged Beauregard sleepily and said, "Go on, boy. Go over there and sleep with Foxy. He needs some warming. Go on!"

Beauregard wouldn't move, either, so Clay resigned himself to the situation. At least, he thought before sleep overtook him, I guess he's earned the right to be called Dan'l, if that's the name he favors. Clay smiled one last sleepy smile. *Dan'l in that lions' den.*

It was strangely fitting.

7

LIKE A BRIGHT-ORANGE BUTTERFLY, the plan to call Foxy by his preferred name flitted through Clay's mind at times, but nothing came of it. In the end, mainly through force of habit, he continued to call him Foxy.

One day, beyond a little town called Dublin, the boys stopped at a huge boulder beside the glistening tracks. Leaning against the warm rock, Clay sniffed the mellow air and watched a green lizard dart to and fro.

"See that lizard," said Clay dreamily. "He knows spring is coming."

Foxy sniffed the air, then glanced longingly to a small stream down a bank. It glistened with patches of sunshine, and soft green buds could be seen about the trees. "You don't reckon we could stop a while?" he asked. "My feet are plumb wore out, and I been hankering for a taste of fish."

While Clay was considering, a trout broke the water.

"Look!" shouted Foxy, "There's one now!"

Clay too had seen the beautiful, inviting arch of the fish against the greening bank. It would be about an hour or longer before they would have to look out for a patrol, since a trainful of soldiers had clanged and chugged through just a few minutes before. It would probably be safe enough.

"All right," said Clay, leading Lazy Girl down the sun-warmed bank toward the stream. "You get out the frying pan just in case."

They walked over the spongy moss-covered ground beside the stream until they came to a shaded spot well out of sight of the railroad. Clay sat on a rock and untied his rawhide bootlaces. He tied them together securely, then asked Foxy for his.

"What do you want with them?" asked Foxy.

"Didn't you go and lose that ball of fishing string you had in your pack? We gotta have line, ain't we?"

"Sure, that's a fine idea," said Foxy. He started to undo his own bootlaces.

Clay took them and tied them to his own, making a long stout line. Then he scratched his head, wondering what they could use for a leader, something to tie the hook to. When Lazy Girl stomped her feet restlessly, he got an idea.

"Come on," he said. "Help me get four long hairs from Lazy Girl's tail. We'll braid them together and they'll do to tie the hook onto."

They secured four long, shiny hairs and braided them together. Then Clay took a fishing hook from his hat and tied it to the hair leader. He tied this to the heavier line.

"Now," he said, grinning, "we'll just see how hungry them fish is!"

Clay's long fingers prodded a while in some rotten wood and soon he came up with half a dozen wriggling white grubworms. He put one of the worms on his hook, dropped the rest into his waist pouch, and pulled the drawstring tight. At last he dropped his line into the swift water.

For a few minutes Clay concentrated on the line. Slowly, in spite of himself, he let his senses soak in the beauty of the first really warm day since they had started. He heard crows cawing over distant treetops and spring peepers shrilling.

64

Presently there was a strike, and a beautiful brook trout, greenish-blue speckled with bright blue and white spots, caught the sun's rays—arched like all the brook trout in the whole world hungry for steel.

"Easy . . . easy . . ." cautioned Clay as his hands slowly, slowly brought in the line, then let it out again . . . playing the frisky fish . . . letting it wear itself out. Finally, when the fish was played out, he directed Foxy to catch it.

"What do I catch it with?" asked Foxy.

"With the two good hands God gave you," he said. "Unless you just happen to have a gunnysack with you!"

Foxy kicked off his boots and splashed into the cold water. Carefully and with a skill that surprised Clay, he scooped up the fish with his hands and threw it up on the bank.

"That's sure some fish," said Foxy. "Why, must be ten inches long, maybe more."

"That it is," smiled Clay.

Clay continued to get strikes, and before the braided lead line finally snapped, he had landed, with the help of Foxy, two large brook trout and a sucker.

"Oh, well," said Clay, philosophical about the lost hook. "We got more hooks, and we got us a good-size meal. Mustn't catch more than we need. It ain't right."

While their fish sizzled, the boys leaned back against the bank and contemplated the perfect vault of blue above. They heard a lonely railroad whistle way off, but they were unprepared for the sudden, cheerful "Hello!" that greeted them from the bank above.

Clay jerked upright and reached for his gun. Foxy scrambled to his feet.

"Any luck, fellows?" asked the intruder, a tall, prematurely gray man with a ruddy complexion. "My, I see you've done quite well for yourselves. May I join you?"

Without waiting for an answer, the man hobbled down the bank—Clay noticed he had a bad limp in his right leg—dusted off a rock with a clean white handkerchief and sat down. He was a well-built man dressed in a fine suit of clothes, and he wore a buckskin jacket and new boots. A bulky pack was strapped to his back.

"How long you boys been fishing?"

When they did not answer right away, he introduced himself, "I'm Doc Meridith, the button and thread man. Would have my entire wagon and horse outfit with me, but some renegade soldier took off with it when my back was turned. I'll catch up to that rascal yet."

"You're not with the railroad?" asked Foxy.

"No, I'm a traveling merchant. Some folks call me the Happy Sutler. Cover the whole land from north to south and back again." He undid the straps of his pack and let it drop to the ground. Then he wiped his brow with the handkerchief. "Anything you gentlemen need? I've got thread and needles for mending . . . fishhooks . . . salt, tobacco . . . dime novels."

"No," said Clay. "We got enough."

"Well," he said with a shrug, "I'll do a thriving business when we get into Lynchburg, if I can beat Sheridan's cavalry. Going to establish my modest headquarters there for a day or so. Those Rebel boys will be happy to see old Doc, and that's a solid-gold fact."

Clay looked at the peddler with caution. He never warmed to strangers, and this one made him more wary than usual. For one thing, he was dressed too well for an ordinary sutler, and he was suspiciously friendly.

"We close to Lynchburg?" asked Foxy.

"Yes, my lads, we are indeed. Are you boys traveling along this bountiful path provided by the railroad?"

Clay's face grew hot.

"Don't be afraid to admit it. I've had reports on you since the last two towns." When the boys showed their astonishment, the merchant explained. "You see, I've got my sources for information. Mighty valuable sometimes, I declare, but—" he broke off and looked longingly toward the sizzling fish. "Mind if I partake of the noon sustenance with you?"

Clay nodded.

"I thank you most kindly."

"Are you a Reb or a Yank?" asked Clay.

Doc laughed and slapped his thigh. "That, my young man, is a highly interesting question. Yes, indeed." He pulled a gray kepi hat from a small bag in his pack and placed it on his head. "I was born in Biloxi, Mississippi, and when I wear this hat, as you can plainly see, I'm a Johnny Reb." Then he withdrew a blue Union hat and put it on. "When I wear this, gentlemen, I'm a true-blooded Union boy, stars and bars all the way." He winked. "It's a help to business and that's a solid-gold fact."

Clay moved uncomfortably and turned the fish.

"I shock you, don't I?" the man asked Clay.

"No . . . I . . ."

"But yes, I can tell." He bent close and sniffed the fish. "Not too done for me, please." He sat back again. "You shouldn't be—shocked, I mean. There is something valuable I learned a long time ago, at my Mammy's knee, in fact —in this life it's got to be every man for himself. Ah, you see patriotism, or what they call patriotism, has no place in the scheme of things. It's a cheap delusion taught us by men who play at war and wear pretty braid on their uniforms."

Clay and Foxy exchanged glances. Clay gave the fish a final turn and scooped it onto three tin plates.

"Ah, well," said the sutler, "you boys probably don't agree, or even know what I'm talking about—not really, but it doesn't matter." He took a bite of his fish and sighed contentedly. "This day is a jewel. The food is beyond compare. And we've a lovely road ahead."

"I'm—I mean, we may not be going to Lynchburg," said Clay.

"Certainly you are—that's been your route so far." The sutler winked. "This railroad doesn't go anywhere else. According to my best information." He turned suddenly to Foxy. "You a runaway?"

"My name is Foxy," the boy said quickly, "and his name is Clay. And we are on our way to Washington City."

Surprisingly, the Doc didn't ask them why, nor pursue the matter as to whether Foxy was a runaway, but he gave them some information that Clay considered useful.

"I have it on good authority," he said, "that Sheridan has captured Early's entire Rebel command between Staunton and Charlottesville, and that he plans to go to Charlottesville and start to rip up the railroad all the way back toward Lynchburg."

Clay tensed. "But we planned to follow the line up to Charlottesville."

"I figured you were," said the merchant. "That's why I told you. As a matter of fact," he added, "I have it on the best authority that Thomas has directed Stoneman to repeat the raid of last fall, destroying the East Tennessee and Virginia—this very line—as far from Knoxville toward Lynchburg as he can."

Clay drew a sharp breath.

"That means," said the Doc, "that any day now, they'll move out from Knoxville to start their diabolical work."

Foxy's eyes were big. "But if we can't go north, we'll have to cut directly east and then . . ."

"Clever lad," said the sutler, smiling. "You'd have to go toward Petersburg."

68

Clay felt a thrill of excitement. What if they had to go that way—by Petersburg . . . and Richmond. Why, they'd run right smack into the fighting!

The sutler, seeming to sense what Clay was thinking, hastened to add, "Don't go getting any grandiose ideas about becoming a hero. War's not for babies." He fished a cheroot from his vest and lighted it, studying Clay thoughtfully. "How old are you, anyway?"

Clay said quickly, "Thirteen . . . be fourteen in June."

"You're big for your age."

Clay nodded.

"And you?"

"I'm twelve," said Foxy. "But I'm strong for my age."

"Not strong enough to withstand Petersburg," said the merchant. "Tell you what. You boys go along with me as far as Lynchburg, then I'll help map out a safe route for you from there."

Clay was ready to think of some excuse when, suddenly, the bushes behind them parted and three bayoneted guns were leveled at them. Behind the guns stood three grim-faced soldiers.

Coming up behind the soldiers was a young lieutenant with red hair, who said, "Well, if it ain't the two boys we been looking for. What you doing along this railroad—planning to blow it up?" He turned then to his men and ordered, "Search 'em . . . and take that rifle."

"Wait a minute, boys," said the Doc amiably. "You're making a mistake. These boys aren't criminals."

"Why, if it ain't the Doc!" grinned the lieutenant. "Didn't recognize you without your wagon!"

The sutler smiled apologetically and shrugged. "Some renegade took my outfit back at Columbia."

The lieutenant laughed heartily. "Well, if that don't beat all! Last time I saw you, you was so loaded with stuff you looked like you'd confiscated half the supplies in the Richmond warehouses!"

The Doc took a long puff on his cigar, inhaled, then said pleasantly, "Anything you boys need? I've still got a few dime novels, some tobacco . . ."

"Say, I could use some tobacco," said the lieutenant. "If it don't beat all, running into you here." He stopped smiling and stared in the direction of the boys. "Wait a minute. What are they doing with you? These boys have been ducking our patrols ever since Greeneville."

Clay shifted his feet. "We—uh—on our way to—"

"Wait a minute," said the sutler, handing the lieutenant a cigar. "Don't hurt these lads. They're good boys. They're working for me, in fact."

"Working for you?"

"Yes, indeed. They're my new helpers. Going to help me set up business in Lynchburg."

"That a fact?" the lieutenant asked Clay.

Clay nodded absently.

"What you got in that pack?" he asked, looking to where Lazy Girl was tied.

"Why," said Clay, "just blankets and cooking pans and . . ."

"They're all right," said the sutler. "I'll vouch for them. This is Clay . . . and that's Foxy."

The lieutenant acknowledged the introduction with a nod of his head, then looked at Foxy with narrowed eyes.

"You a runaway?"

Foxy, now looking frightened, opened his mouth to answer, but the sutler answered quickly, "No, of course not. He's got his freedom. Wouldn't be with me, otherwise."

"And you," he said, looking to Clay, "how old are you?"

"Be fourteen in June," said Clay.

70

The officer looked at him thoughtfully. "Can you prove it?"

"It's in my family Bible," said Clay.

"Come now, lieutenant," said the Doc. "Since when did you boys start robbing the cradle? Can't you see this boy ain't even got peach fuzz on his upper lip yet?"

"Looks big enough to carry a gun to me," said the lieutenant. "I ought to swear him in right here."

Clay stiffened.

"Come, fellows," said the sutler. "Help us finish up this delicious fish dinner, then I'll get you some tobacco from my pack."

The soldiers dived into the remaining fish with such relish that Clay figured they hadn't eaten in a long time. One of them even rubbed two fingers along the sides of the skillet, then licked the fingers. Clay had heard that in the Reb camps there was terrible hunger and sickness, but until then it hadn't seemed quite real to him. One of the soldiers, a tall, thin man with pale skin and an ill-fitting uniform, looked as though he shouldn't even be on his feet.

Walking back along the railroad, Clay breathed a sigh of relief. For so many days he and Foxy had dreaded meeting the patrol. Danger had hung over them like a dark cloud, making them tense to every twig creaking, to every tree rustle.

Now that they had been discovered and they had been saved—at least for the moment—by the sutler, Clay could breathe more easily.

While the sutler talked with the lieutenant up ahead, Clay hung back and started to talk with one of the soldiers.

"Seems like everybody knows the Doc," said Clay.

"Yeah," laughed the soldier. "He 'pears to pop up all over the place. Like a bad penny."

"I wonder how he gets around so much," mused Clay.

The soldier looked at him with surprise, "Why, didn't you know? Sometimes even the gen'rls give him transport from one place to another."

Clay was surprised. "I ain't been with him long enough to—"

"He's sure in with the high command."

"A sutler," said Clay. "Why, it don't even make sense."

The soldier laughed. "You sure ain't been with him long, I can see that. You'll find out soon enough, I guess."

"Find out what?"

"That he's a spy."

So great was his surprise, Clay almost stumbled. "A—*what?*"

"Sure, he collects information while he's selling his trinkets . . . some of it mighty useful, I reckon."

"But if he's a spy for the South . . ."

The soldier laughed again. "I didn't say that. I said he was a spy."

Clay swallowed hard. "You mean . . . is he . . ."

"Sells information to both sides, he does," said the soldier. "Though it 'pears at times he favors the South. Reckon he was born South."

This was almost too much for Clay to swallow. A traveling merchant who was a spy was not too hard to believe or understand. But for him to sell information to both sides! And for both sides apparently to allow him to come and go. There seemed to be something terrible wrong . . .

"But how could they let him come and go in their camps, when they know—"

The soldier shifted his gun to his other shoulder and grunted. "Ain't you never heard the sayin' 'Don't cut off your nose to spite your face'? I reckon that's the way they figure with the Doc."

72

Clay tried to sort it out in his confused mind. It was a strange war, indeed. He looked ahead to the tracks glistening blindingly in the sun, to the sutler. He was talking with the redheaded lieutenant, limping along beside him.

He's a strange one, thought Clay sharply, a real strange one.

8

THE CAMP AT LYNCHBURG was a dismal place. The huts, in long monotonous rows, were built of logs, mud, and wood slabs. Barrels and rusty pipes served for chimneys. The men, lean and dressed not much better than scarecrows, gathered about in knots, when not doing duties, and talked longingly of home. Sometimes they sang halfheartedly, and sometimes they played cards or read. But mostly they just sat as though they were waiting for something.

And everywhere was mud and filth.

Clay was shocked when he looked into the faces of the soldiers. They stared back with hollow eyes that had forgotten how to smile. The wounded hobbled around on crutches, or sat inside their huts, staring ahead aimlessly.

It broke Clay's heart, for he still remembered his Pa saying how the South was going to win because it had the most spirit. He had to pinch himself to realize that these men, long-faced and thin and pale, were the invincible South that had marched into battle proudly wearing the Rebel gray.

That gray was tattered now. Some of the men wore gray, some uniforms of butternut homespun, some wore part gray, part Union blue taken from dead Union soldiers on the battlefield. Boots, what were left of them, resembled mud-caked strips of leather, and many still had their feet wrapped in blanket strips from winter.

But the sitting and waiting bothered Clay almost more than anything else.

"It's heartbreaking," agreed Doc when Clay mentioned this. "There's no spirit left. They're just waiting now for the war to be over so they can go home."

When Clay finished helping the sutler set up his tent, he asked, "Do you think it will be over soon?"

Doc sat on an empty crate, his bad leg stretched out in front of him, and lighted one of his cheroots. "It's hard to say. Looks like General Lee's having a bad time of it at Petersburg." He gazed off absently. Then, after a long while, he said, "You know, Clay, Petersburg is the key to the whole thing. You see, it supplies material and food to Richmond. Keeps Richmond alive. Protects it too. Without Petersburg . . . well, that's the end of Richmond." He picked up a stick and drew in the mud. "Right now, the Union boys have a noose around Lee's neck. See, here's Petersburg, and here's the Reb entrenchments." He drew another line below the first one. "And this long encircling line is the Union entrenchment. You understand?"

Clay wasn't quite sure, but he nodded.

"It looks bad," Doc said, staring off and puffing big clouds of smoke. When he spoke again, he stood up and his voice went soft. "If there was only a way for Lee to break through the line . . . here . . . or here, say on the Danville Road. Maybe he could regroup some of his forces at a point farther south and . . ."

"You mean," said Clay hopefully, "there's still a chance?"

Doc laughed and sat back again. "Never underestimate the shrewdness of Robert E. Lee. There's a smart man and

75

a gentleman to boot! He might find a way to shake off that old noose yet!"

"But if he gives up Petersburg, what about Richmond?"

The sutler frowned. "Yes, that's the difficult part. But who knows, maybe old Jeff Davis can move the capital someplace else. All things are possible, remember that."

There was a lot of wishful thinking in the sutler's talk, and this seemed strange to Clay. He knew, too, from things the Doc had said that he didn't favor the Southern cause. In fact, he had told them, "Slavery is wrong. No man should be a slave to another. And that old saying 'No nation can be half slave and half free' is true as any words ever spoken."

Yet the Doc seemed to be pulling for the South. Maybe, in spite of all his fancy words about patriotism being so much hogwash, he still felt some strong attachment to the land that gave him his birth. Or maybe it was his strong liking for the tall, stately Lee, who, Doc had said, was "the greatest soldier in all history."

"Or maybe," Clay said later to Foxy, "he just wants to see the losing side put up a danged good fight before going down."

" 'Pears to me," said Foxy, "that ole Doc's like a pretty plantation gal, always changin' her mind about which feller she wants to take her courtin'."

Clay, in spite of his gloomy feelings, had to laugh.

For two days the sutler did a brisk business. A courier, a tall man dressed in western garb, rode into camp one evening with a wagonload of fresh supplies for the sutler. They talked a while, him and Doc, and then he drove off.

The soldiers in camp were short on barter items. Some indeed seemed to have nothing but one blanket, a canteen, a knife, and a cartridge box. Some didn't even have that much. But they had saved much of their $18-a-month pay, and they pushed so much Confederate money at the sutler and the boys that Clay began to feel like a fancy banker.

"Don't let all that money fool you," said the Doc. "It ain't worth too much more than the paper it's printed on."

At night, when there seemed nothing to do but gather around a campfire and talk, the Doc told the soldiers stories about the war and the men listened eagerly, each one pitifully anxious to hear some word about his home town.

In their own tent, the sutler told the boys some of his personal experiences. He told how, as a young boy, he had had a bad fall from his favorite horse, Vicki, and how he had almost lost his right leg. How the injury had kept him out of serving in the army. He told how he had risked his life at Shiloh, carrying a wounded soldier to safety after he had been hit with a Minié ball.

"That boy had half his guts blown out," he said, "and he was as brave as you could want. I got him to a doctor and the doc took him into this farmhouse, put him on a kitchen table, cleaned off his insides, shoved them back in and sewed him up neat as a pin."

"What happened to him?" asked Foxy.

"Why, he went right back to fighting, of course!"

"Was he a Reb or a Yankee?" asked Clay.

The Doc laughed. "What difference does that make? There were a lot of brave ones on both sides."

That night in the tent Clay listened to the chill March wind blowing across the land, and he thought about the wind complaining beneath the eaves of his cabin on the ridge. How he would love to be there now, sitting in his squeaky old rocker whittling or rustling up a squirrel stew.

What the sutler had said kept coming back to him. What made him like he was? It wasn't so much the words he was always saying—it was his feelings behind the words that

Clay read. Clay's Ma always told him she could "read a body's feelings," and Clay felt he had this gift.

He decided, before he and Bory fell asleep on the cot, that the Doc, changeable as he was, was wishing he could have worn a gray uniform and a jaunty kepi hat. He would have done General Robert E. Lee proud.

On the next sunrise, Clay had decided, they would depart for the last leg of their journey to Washington. He was hankering more than ever to see Clem, and he felt it was time to move on. Lazy Girl had had a good rest and he and Foxy had sewn up all the rips in their clothes.

He told the Doc, and the Doc promised that if they would stay just one more day, he would map out a safe route and see them on their way.

"Just stay the day," said the sutler, "and tomorrow morning, bright and early, I'll see you off. I'll be shoving on myself soon."

Clay finally agreed and spent most of the day checking things they would put in their pack and studying the map that Doc drew for them. He couldn't read the names of the towns and rivers Doc had marked, but he could tell from listening to him which way they should go.

The route would take them up along the east side of the James River, to Columbia. From Columbia they would cut cross-country to Trevillian, then up to Fredericksburg.

Doc showed them a place where they could cross the James River at a bridge, getting into Columbia, and explained which roads would be best to travel from there.

"You're fine boys," said the sutler, "and it's been a pleasure knowing both of you. Wish I could go along with you."

Clay wished he could too. He had grown to like the strange, unpredictable man.

That evening, while Clay was tending Lazy Girl in the

corral, he heard confusion and laughter in the camp. He hurried back to the sutler's tent and there he found some of the men taunting Foxy. One of the soldiers that the others called Slim was ordering Foxy to shine his shoes.

"But, Mister Slim," Foxy was saying, shaking his head, "them shoes ain't—"

"Ain't what?" demanded the tall, thin soldier with the dark shrewd eyes. "Are you trying to tell me they ain't good enough to shine?"

Clay looked to the man's feet. The shoes were not much more than scraps of leather held together with thin, knotted string, and so encrusted with mud you could scarcely tell where the shoes ended and the man's feet began.

"Yessuh, but I—"

"Don't 'yessuh' me. Just you get something and shine them shoes." Slim turned to the others and winked. "The colonel himself is waiting to have supper with me, and I got to look purty!"

Foxy went into the sutler's tent and presently came out with a dirty cloth and a bent spoon. He leaned over the soldier's feet and tried, painstakingly, to scrape off some of the filth.

The soldier, enjoying the attention he was getting from onlookers, suddenly jerked his foot up and sent Foxy sprawling backward into a mudhole.

Clay felt a stab of anger, but he was afraid to move. He stood rooted to the spot and waited to see what Foxy would do. Foxy wasn't afraid—at least he didn't think he was, but there were so many of them. Sometimes a crowd could be mean as a pack of she-wolves.

"Aw, cut it out. Leave the kid alone," one soldier yelled. But others egged him on. "That's the way, Slim—put him in his place."

Foxy stood up with great dignity, wiped some of the mud

from himself and went back to scraping dirt from the soldier's shoes.

Clay looked around frantically for the Doc, but he was nowhere in sight. Just then he heard a fresh uproar of laughter and looked to see Foxy again sprawled in the mud, a thin line of blood trickling from his mouth this time.

"Leave him be!" yelled one of the men. "He's just a kid, for God's sake!"

Clay wanted to make the soldier stop. But there were so many of them, and their voices were high-pitched and excited. Most of them were not in any reasoning mood.

Clay felt helpless.

But when Bory came up to him, whining, Clay ordered, "Get him, Bory! Get him!"

Teeth bared like a she-wolf, Bory rushed the soldier and sent him sprawling in the mudhole alongside Foxy. The men laughed louder than ever, but the soldier was fighting mad now. His eyes were cruel slits. "I'll kill that dog!" he threatened in an ugly voice, trying to hold the growling dog off. Clay feared that he would, given the chance.

Clay grabbed his hunting rifle and leveled it at the soldier's head. "You—touch—one—hair on that dog and I'll . . ."

The soldier stared at Clay in surprise. "What are you anyway?" he asked, spitting out each word slowly and distinctly. "You some kind of white—"

"Evening, fellows," said the Doc, suddenly appearing on the scene. "Having a little evening sport and recreation?"

The soldier turned his glare from Clay to stare at the sutler. The Doc calmly took a cheroot from his pocket and lighted it, taking his time about it. "Say . . . since we're all in such a celebrating mood, why don't you boys just step up to my tent and I'll give out a little free tobacco."

The change that came over the place was electric.

80

"Tobacco!" went up the cry like a signal, and suddenly there was a stampede.

"Quick," said the Doc to Clay, "get Foxy and Beauregard out of here. I'll take care of the muddy one."

In the general confusion, Clay grabbed Bory and whispered to Foxy that he should follow him. As the boys took off, Clay looked back to see the Doc bending over the soldier, giving him a hand up out of the mudhole.

"Jiminy and thunder," breathed Clay at last when they were a way outside the camp, "that was a close one!"

"Yeah," said Foxy. "If it hadn't been for you, and Bory, and the Doc . . ."

Emotions—fear, the old bitter resentment, shame too, and a feeling of uneasiness—surged through Clay all at the same time, and he snapped, "Don't thank me! Just stay out of trouble for a while if you can!"

9

CLAY AWOKE during the night. He was aware of a sound, and at first he thought it was a noise in his dream. Then he realized it was someone talking. Two men talking outside the sutler's tent where he slept.

He strained to listen.

Presently he could make out one of the voices—it was the Doc's. The other was more high-pitched and twangy. A voice he did not know.

Listening hard, he could make out a few words. He heard "Petersburg" and "Southside" and a question: "How big is the cannon?" The question was asked by the Doc. But he couldn't make out the other's answer. Nor did he know which cannon the sutler was asking about. He thought, too, he heard General Lee's name, then General Beauregard's.

Thinking it might be some important information about the war, Clay listened more closely. But presently the men moved away from the tent, and he could hear nothing more than a soft murmur of their voices, rising and falling like the wind. He waited, hoping they would move back closer to the tent. But they did not. He lay for a long time, his ears straining, but all he could hear finally was Foxy's heavy breathing from the next cot, the wind whining, the cracking sound of canvas flapping, and a dog barking somewhere off in the distance.

The wind howled louder, and soon the howling mixed with a hypnotizing plop-plop of rain on the tent roof. Clay pulled his warm blankets closer, patted Bory, and went back to sleep.

At dawn, when the bugler's reveille struck its high notes and the tones echoed through the camp, quivered, hung in the air, and stirred his cocoon of sleep, Foxy was shaking him and saying, "Mister Clay, wake up! The Doc ain't here no more. He's gone!"

Clay sat up and rubbed his eyes. "What do you mean? Maybe he's just—"

"No, he's gone," said Foxy. " 'Cause the blankets is gone from his bed and that pack he always carried with him."

Clay opened his eyes wider. There, on the far floor of the tent, beside the sutler's cot, where he had put it, was Lazy Girl's pack, but none of the sutler's things were there. The bed was stripped clean of bedcovers and his pack was missing. None of his personal belongings remained.

Clay suddenly remembered the conversation he had heard during the night. It must have been something important to make the Doc leave so suddenly, without even saying good-by.

Clay dressed and went outside. He asked a sentry if he had seen the Doc.

The soldier, who looked dead on his feet, said sleepily, "Yeah, he went off that way." His long arm pointed toward a road, misty now in the early light, which Clay knew led to Petersburg. He remembered the word "Petersburg" in the talking he had overheard. Yes, that's where Doc would be going, although Clay had not heard enough of the conversation to know why.

He was disappointed. He had hoped to see his friend

83

once more before he and Foxy departed that morning. He wanted to thank the Doc, too, for the fine map he had made for them.

"Oh, well," Clay shrugged, turning away, "maybe he had something important—"

"He sure must have," laughed the sentry, his smile reflecting back the pale rosy light, "the way he was tickling the ribs of that poor mule!"

Clay jerked around.

"Mule!"

"Yeah," said the soldier, "the way he was riding that animal, you'da thought he had a message for the general himself!" He snorted. "That—or he thought mebbe the devil was after him."

Clay's heart sank. He *couldn't* . . . not Lazy Girl!

He turned and ran through the camp toward the corral and barns. His heart pumped wildly. Unmindful of mudholes and men coming and going, he rushed headlong, thinking only one thought, a prayer, really.

"Hey—watch where you're going!" some of the men shouted at him and then turned to watch in surprise.

When Clay reached the corral, he found a long line of skinny army horses, with a sentry throwing them hay. Lazy Girl was not in her usual place.

He pointed to the spot where she had been tied. "Where's the mule!" he demanded, breathless. "The one that was tied here?"

The soldier looked up, with a blank face at first. At last recognizing Clay, he smiled. "Why, your friend saddled her and took her, said you knew all about it."

"Oh, no!" groaned Clay. "He *couldn't!*"

"What's the matter, son?"

"Don't you see," pleaded Clay in a desperate voice.

84

"That's *my* mule . . . my Pa give her to me. He couldn't take her . . . not Lazy Girl!"

The soldier shrugged and went back to feeding the gaunt horses. "That's tough, kid, but he shore wasn't 'llowed to take none of these. These is Confederate Army."

Clay hurried to the front gate of the camp, near the sutler's tent. He grabbed the sentry he had talked to before. "Please," he said, his fingers imploring, digging into the sleeve of the uniform, "where did he go? Did he say?"

"I told you," said the soldier, shaking off Clay's hand. "He rode off that way." He thought for a minute. "And, nope, he didn't say nothing."

Fighting back tears, Clay ran out onto the lonely, gray road in the direction the soldier had pointed. He ran without thinking, blindly, his jacket flapping in the wind. The wind whipped his face and it was cold. A light mist came down in his face and settled in his hair like dew.

The road was quite deserted, and the dawn picked out rose-hued trees alongside and little gullies, and birds stirring in the uppermost branches. Of all these things, Clay was hardly aware. He was only conscious of one thing—he had to catch up to the sutler. He had to get Lazy Girl back. Somehow.

He ran and ran until he felt a burning in his throat. He ran until his lungs felt ready to burst. But he willed his long legs to run faster, to eat up as much road between him and the sutler as possible.

He wanted to cry, felt the need to cry. But he held back tears angrily. He needed all his strength for running.

Presently, at one place in the road, he came upon an unexpected hole. His foot twisted under him and brought him down, making him strike the ground with such force it knocked the wind from his lungs.

85

Dizzily, he felt the pain. It came like a stab of fire in his ankle at first, then an all-consuming, throbbing, aching all over, spreading up through his leg and his entire body.

He grabbed the ankle with his hands and squeezed until his knuckles went white. Holding the injured ankle like that, he tried to put weight on it. It gave way under him and he sank back to the ground.

He looked down the road. There was no sign of human life. Only the birds greeting the gray, rosy-pink dawn, huddling beneath tree limbs to protect their feathers from the peppering rain. Chipmunks scurried here and there. Raindrops glistened from trees and bushes like diamonds. He listened. No sounds came except the twittering of the birds.

Clay reached to his face and wiped away something sticky and wet from his mouth. Looking at his hand, he saw blood streaked with dirt. But this did not hurt, not like the throbbing, pulsating pain in his ankle. He felt helpless, lying there letting the waves of pain sweep over him, straining to see down the road where they had gone, sensing the futility of trying to catch them now.

The emptiness.

He laid his head on the wet earth and breathed deep of its damp, rich, familiar smell. He moaned, and in that moan, compounded of despair, loneliness, frustration, pain, the hurt of losing something you love, the uncertainty of his mission—the agony of life itself—came one word. That word echoed and reverberated through the glistening, budding woods, down the empty road and up to the morning sky like a prayer . . . "Pa!"

Back in camp, a kindly, white-haired doctor taped up Clay's ankle and reminded him how lucky he was. "It's not broken," he said, "but it's a mighty ugly sprain. You'd be smart to rest up for a few days . . . stay off of it as much as possible."

"But I have to go after my mule," said Clay, hoping the man would understand. "If we leave today, maybe we can catch up—"

The doctor shook his head. "I know how you feel, son, but believe me, it's not worth the risk. If you hurt that foot again, you could do permanent harm to it."

Clay was resolute. "I have to get to Petersburg somehow," he said. "I have to find my mule."

"All right," said the doctor, "if you're so determined. But at least, get someone to fix you up with a pair of crutches." He smiled apologetically and shrugged. "I'd give you a pair myself, but you see, we're terribly short of—"

"I understand," said Clay quickly. "I thank you for all you've done."

Foxy went into the woods and brought back two stout sticks with forked tops. They tore up old rags into strips and carefully padded the forks. Clay found that by gripping the sticks tightly with his hands, he could hobble about in a fairly satisfactory way—a sort of hopping, walking gait.

He and Foxy gathered together as much of their supplies as they could carry on their backs and started out. Foxy carried Clay's rifle and his sword. They had to leave some blankets, the ax, and many of their cooking utensils behind.

"Mister Clay," Foxy said, shaking his head, "I don't like you trying to walk with that busted ankle. I wish you'd wait another day or more. They'd let us stay."

"No," said Clay. "I've got to hurry if we're going to catch up with him. He's known by many a soldier hereabouts. Maybe we can ask as we go along. I'm sure he's headed for Petersburg."

And so they traveled much of that morning. Clay hobbled beside the boy. His armpits ached after a while, but he said nothing of this. He tried not to think of the pain. He tried to think of what he had to do.

Finally the dirt road they were traveling led into a plank road, but Clay had trouble keeping the tips of the sticks from becoming wedged between the cracks. Once, when he couldn't dislodge the crutch quickly enough, he fell forward, jarring his bad ankle. He lay on the road a few minutes, letting waves of pain wash over him.

After they had lunch beside the road, an old farmer came along in a wagon and offered them a ride. Gratefully, Clay climbed into the wagon bed, with Foxy's help, and they rode as far as Appomattox Court House.

When the farmer let them out, Clay and Foxy thanked him.

The old man shook his head. "Sure you young'uns want to go all the way to Petersburg?"

Clay nodded.

"Don't you know they's fightin' there?"

Clay nodded again.

The old man looked at Clay's ankle and shrugged. "Well," he drawled, "it ain't no business of mine. Just hope you know what you're about."

Clay thanked him again as he hobbled off, and the farmer called after them, wishing them good luck.

By the time they had gone a little way out of Appomattox Court House, Clay's ankle had swollen so badly they had to stop and loosen his boot again. The skin was bluish and bulging around the edges of the tight bandaging.

Foxy frowned. "Mister Clay, we better stop now. I'll fix us up a lean-to and build a fire."

"No," said Clay stubbornly. "We'll keep going as long as we can."

Finally, when it was so dark they could no longer see the road, Foxy persuaded Clay to stop and build a fire. Soon he had a mess of beans cooking and some corn bread. Clay lay back on some pine needles Foxy had fixed for him and smiled. "You might make a pretty good woodsman yet," he said, and Foxy grinned.

The next morning Clay's foot was worse, but he insisted on starting out bright and early. He had trouble with the crutches again, and once, going over a little bridge, his crutch got wedged in between the planks and he pitched forward again. This time bright stars exploded before his eyes and he almost passed out from the pain. Rubbing the stars away with his fists, he struggled to get up. Bory whimpered as Foxy helped him to his feet.

"Mister Clay," said Foxy, "you can't go on like this. You gotta rest a while. Here, I'll help you to that little clearing beside the road, and I'll find you some more sticks. Something bigger at the bottom so they won't get stuck in them places in the road."

"All right," said Clay reluctantly. "We'll rest, but just a little while."

While Clay rested, Foxy went off into the woods to look for new sticks. He was gone a long time and Clay started to doze. His face felt feverish, and he supposed a little nap wouldn't hurt. When he opened his eyes again, Foxy was standing before him, grinning.

"What are you so happy about?" asked Clay. "Did you find some better crutches?"

Foxy shook his head. "No, but I got something better!"

"Better?"

Foxy smiled and started to help him up.

"You'll see. You just come with me."

Foxy led him off into a thicket, toward a thick verge of woods.

"Wait a minute," complained Clay. "You're leading us way off the road!"

"Never you mind," said Foxy smugly. "You'll see pretty soon. It's a surprise!"

They went along through the woods until they came to a big rock jutting out over a river. The river flowed swiftly, and Clay could tell at a glance it threatened to rise up over its banks.

"What place is this?" asked Clay. "Why did you—"

"This," said Foxy importantly, "is the Ap-po-mattox River. It flows down that way . . . down toward where it meets up with the James. Then it flows nice as you please, right out to the ocean."

Clay snorted. "You mean to tell me you brought me all the way here to give me a lesson in *geography!* He eyed Foxy suspiciously. And how'd you learn all that any—"

"While you was sleeping, I found me some field hands, working over there in that big field. I talked to their boss man and he took a mighty fine liking to that sword of mine . . ."

Clay looked quickly to where the sword usually swung from Foxy's belt. It was not there.

"Your sword! What did you do with it?"

"I traded it."

"For—"

"For that," Foxy said proudly, pointing down the bank to where a raft lay anchored to the big rock. The raft, made of crudely cut planks, was lashed together with bits of rope, some of it badly frayed. It was uneven on the surface and looked as though it might break apart at any moment.

"Ain't it purty?" asked Foxy. "All we have to do now is get you down this here bank and . . ."

"You mean we can follow this river all the way to Petersburg?"

Foxy nodded. "I figure we can travel better this way, with that bad ankle of yours, and maybe we can beat that old Doc after all, get there before him."

Clay marveled at Foxy's strategy.

"You *sure* this winds up at Petersburg?"

"That's what my friends over there in that big field say. The river, its all swelled up now from rain, but if we be careful . . ."

Clay sighed. He knew how much Foxy had loved his sword. It was the one valuable thing he owned. It must have hurt him to give it up. He remembered, suddenly, how Foxy had toted it so far, carefully hiding it when they went through unfriendly towns, how he had rushed at that mountain lion with it to save Lazy Girl.

A sudden rush of gratitude came over him.

He turned to Foxy, who was waiting for his answer. Putting his arm on Foxy's shoulder so he could steady himself going down the bank to the raft, he grinned. "If you just don't beat all."

10

"THIS OLE RAFT she pitches . . . this old raft she rocks. But by gum we'll get to Pe-ters-burg . . . be-fo' she finally docks!"

Foxy's tuneful attempt to make him look at the brighter side of things only made Clay smile faintly. Normally, the boy's songs cheered him, but now he could think only of the slow, perilous progress they were making and the dull aching pain in his ankle. And the fever steadily rising.

Clay lay back on the raft, dangling his fingertips in the water, and watched Foxy manage the long pole as though he had been born to water. Clay mistrusted the swollen, muddy stream and knew that if they hit a jagged rock, the rope holding the raft together was in danger of snapping. He had never learned to swim, and Foxy had told him he hadn't either.

Into Clay's feverish brain came other worries. There were moccasins, mean snakes with cottony white mouths and curved fangs, that eyed them suspiciously as they slid past. And there were eddies and whirlpools. There were fallen trees, sometimes almost spanning the river in narrow places, and they had to lie flat on their bellies to pass under them. And beaver dams.

Clay lay and watched, half aware of the exposed tree roots jutting into the stream, the early-blooming marsh marigolds and bitter cress, the winter's weeds dull brown and the bright green of the new grass. He saw, through treetops, the metal sun rise high in the sky, wink through bare branches and new foliage, then slowly, slowly dip into the west.

Although it was mid-March now, the wind still bit into their skins, and the dampness of the river seemed to settle in their bones. Clay pulled his collar closer and wondered when warm weather would come again. Nostalgically, he remembered the wonderously warm balmy day when they had stopped along the railroad and fished for trout.

He dozed a lot, and in his light dozing he tried to imagine the joy of finding Lazy Girl. He tried to imagine whether the sutler was feeding her proper, whether he was mistreating her. He knew now something he had not known before. Lazy Girl was not just another mule, an animal to be traded or bartered. Or sold. She was part of his family.

Part of the little family he had left.

He fought sleep as the fever rose. He tried to eat the meager meals, the fish and other things Foxy offered. But food now tasted like paper. Or it had no taste at all.

During their first few days of travel down the river, Foxy would pole the raft into shore at intervals so that they could build a fire and cook. They would find some good clear spot on the bank and rest there. But after a while, they saved a portion of their breakfast to eat for lunch as they continued to travel.

Beauregard was uneasy. He would bark at the snakes and at the beavers that sometimes paddled across in front of them. He padded restlessly back and forth on the small space of their raft.

"Don't worry, Bory," Foxy would say soothingly. "We ain't gonna be on this raft forever."

But to Clay's feverish brain it seemed as though they would. It was always a relief to stop and go ashore for the night, anchoring the raft securely to some rock or shoreline tree. Foxy would help him hobble to a resting place, then he would gather fire tinder. If the weather was too cold or rainy, Foxy would build them shelter of some kind. Otherwise, they would sleep out in the open beneath the bright stars.

One night, lying on a bed of pine boughs, looking up at the heavens, Clay sighed and wondered—for the first time—whether they would really make Petersburg. The river, with its crooks and turns and rapids, and deep places with whirlpools, seemed endless. A path of swirling, muddy water going nowhere.

His face was flushed and his whole body felt afire. He looked at the cool sky and listened to the owls hooting and the frogs' deep croaking. He thought how nice it would be if he could just go to sleep and sleep and sleep.

"Mister Clay, wake up!" Foxy shouted in his ear the next morning. Clay struggled to open his eyes, but it was a terrible effort. When he did get partly awake, he felt only half alive. His body now was consumed with a dry, hot, burning fire, and things went swimming by his vision, and he had no sense of time or place.

"You look terrible bad," Foxy said. "I gotta get us to high, drier ground."

Through a sleepy haze he sensed that Foxy's hands were under his shoulders, pulling him up, struggling to get him up a high, slippery bank. "Come on, Mister Clay . . . keep movin' them big feet—we gotta get you up there on that high ground."

"Leave me be," Clay heard his voice saying. He knew it

must be his voice. But it seemed strangely far away. A voice without a body. Outside himself.

"You must have swamp fever," said Foxy worriedly.

Clay finally realized somehow that he was up on high dry ground and that Foxy was covering him with blankets and that he was shaking violently. First he felt cold, deathly cold. Then in the next few minutes he was hot. Then he felt hot and cold at the same time. He would fling off the blanket and try to escape the fire inside him.

His lips felt parched, and he tried to lick them to give them moisture.

Beauregard, beside him, whimpered, and he tried weakly to pat him.

He remembered Foxy's cool comforting hands, rubbing his head with cold compresses . . . Foxy talking to him, telling him not to worry . . . Foxy urging him to sip some hot tea. The days and nights blurred together and time had no meaning.

Once he was vaguely aware that it was raining, because he could hear the thudding sound of it striking the evergreen boughs that Foxy had fashioned into a protecting cover. And he could feel the cold rain strike his skin when the wind changed direction.

In his delirium one day he imagined that a group of Negro field hands had stopped to talk to Foxy. He could hear their voices clearly, deep, basso voices, and they were saying that they would take Foxy with them, if he wanted to go.

Did he dream it? He wasn't sure.

"We'll help you get to Washington," one of them was saying. "You just come with us."

"I can't leave him," said Foxy. "And you can see he's too sick to travel."

"What you want to worry 'bout him for?" asked one of

them. "He's got the fever and he'll probably die anyway. Leave him and come with us."

The Doc's words came to him from far off. *In this life it's got to be every man for himself. Nobody's going to look out for you.*

Was it a dream or was it real? He tried to come awake, but he was lost in a nightmare of fever, and thoughts and sounds and pictures swirled through his head. He imagined that one of the field hands gave Foxy a handmade wooden spoon, scooped out with a whittling knife, to stir his food.

He slept again and in his dreams Foxy had gone off and left him. He was alone in the woods with nothing to eat and nothing to fish or trap with. The dream took him along a gray, silent road, and then he was standing on a high mountain and it was springtime and he saw miles and miles of azalea and laurel painting the hills everywhere. He could see the mist around the points, and then he was cold and lying beneath a blanket of cold snow.

He was cold and alone.

One morning he awoke and the sun was shining warm on the earth and a nest of robins greeted his awakening in a branch above. The mother robin was flying back and forth with twigs and bits of vine and leaves and the father robin, fat and sassy, was guarding her movements with an anxious eye. He watched them, fascinated, as though he had never before seen this miracle of spring.

Slowly he realized Foxy was cooking something that smelled good over a campfire. He inhaled the food smells and the tangy smell of woodsmoke and opened his eyes wider.

Yes, Foxy was really there. He was wearing his red woolly cap, pushed back now on his head, and his concentration was almost funny. Beauregard was watching him, wagging his tail and looking at him with his down-at-the-corners eyes that never seemed to smile.

Clay ran a tongue over his parched lips and asked in a weak voice, "What you cooking that smells so all-fired good?"

Foxy dropped his spoon and stared at him, as though he didn't believe his eyes, or ears. "Glory be!" shouted Foxy. "You done broke your fever!" He came running to him. "How you feel?"

Clay tried to rise on one elbow. "Better. I think."

"Lay back," said Foxy. "You mighty weak. I'll fix you up some of this here fish stew."

"Fish stew!"

"Sho'—I caught me a nice string of fish in that river and I put in some onion, and some spring water, and then I threw in some sassafras chips . . ."

Clay blinked and wondered if the fever had affected his hearing. "Sassafras! With fish!"

Foxy chuckled. "Listen at that, Bory. Your master's better and that's for sure." He dished up some of the stew and brought it to Clay, who smiled and inhaled deeply before digging in. "If you ain't never tasted it," said Foxy, "how you know it ain't good?"

Clay smiled. "I guess you're right." He sat up. "The way I feel right now, I could eat the whole thing, pot and all!"

Foxy whistled happily as he served Clay another dishful. Clay gobbled down the second helping and said, "That's the finest stew I ever ate. Got any more?"

After a while Foxy brought him a handful of mint-flavored leaves he had picked in the woods.

"What are these?" asked Clay warily.

Foxy shrugged. "Don't know. But I been eatin' 'em for three days and I'm still kicking."

"Three days!" Clay found this hard to believe. It seemed only the day before that he had got sick.

Clay looked around while he chewed the leaves. In addition to the green boughs that protected him overhead, Foxy had dug a little trench all around them to drain off rain and to keep snakes away. Foxy told him he had run out of matches and had been using the flint and steel from Clay's waist pouch.

"It works right good with that dry moss in your pouch," said Foxy. "Why, if them fish'd hold out, we could stay here till doomsday I guess!"

Clay smiled and remembered the time when he had accused the boy of not knowing a thing about the woods.

"Foxy," he said slowly, "I *oughta* call you Dan'l."

Foxy looked up quickly, pleased. "You mean for Dan'l that was in that lions' den?"

"No," Clay said thoughtfully, "for Dan'l Boone."

As they glided downriver again, things seemed easier. The river had gone down an inch or two and the currents didn't seem as swift as before. Clay now helped with the poling, since his ankle was better, and they made good time. Although still weak, he got to where he almost enjoyed the challenge of steering the raft's course around hairpin turns, through floating brush, and over rapids. In the long, smooth stretches he daydreamed.

"You know," said Clay. "This ain't so bad, traveling by water."

"The Indians thought water was the best way," said Foxy, "and my Granny told me they always camped near a stream."

That first night after Clay's recovery, they built a fire and sat near it, soaking up the warmth, and talking. It was warm enough to sleep in the open.

"Do you think about her a lot?" asked Clay. "Your Granny, I mean."

Foxy nodded. "I sure do. My Granny, she was a mighty fine woman. She used to take good care of me."

"I'll bet you miss her."

Foxy didn't answer, but Clay knew there was no need.

"My Granny," Foxy said after a while, "she used to blow warm smoke into my ear when I got the earache, and she give me herbs and poultices when I got the sickness. And she told me stories, and made me laugh when things seemed hard."

Clay didn't ask what the "hard" things were, but he could guess that the life of a slave was none too pleasant.

"When did you decide to run away?" asked Clay. "I mean, wasn't you scairt that they'd catch you and bring you back?"

Foxy didn't answer for a long time. He watched a stick snap in two, and sighed. "Mister Clay, I'm gonna tell you something. I meant to tell you before, only . . ."

"What is it, Foxy?"

Foxy stared hard into the fire, his eyes averting Clay's glance. "Truth is, I ain't no runaway."

Clay sucked in his breath. "You—ain't!"

Foxy continued in a low, garbled voice. "I coulda had my freedom before I decided to strike out for where Mr. Lincoln is, but . . ." He bit his lip and almost buried his chin in his jacket so Clay had to lean forward to catch his words. "The truth is . . . my master he was hard up after the war started going bad . . . and he didn't have no more pigs . . . and he didn't hardly have enough food for his own family." Two tears rolled down Foxy's dusky cheeks and the fire glow transformed them into shimmering pinpoints of light.

Clay looked away, saying, "You don't have to tell me . . ."

"I want you to know. My Granny, she says the truth is a mighty fine thing." He wiped the tears away impatiently, but his voice still sounded almost too low to be heard. "Truth be, Mister Clay, my master he didn't want me no more. I was too little to do heavy work, and he . . . well, he just didn't want me 'round."

Clay knew the rest. He knew, without Foxy saying it, that the boy wanted, like everyone, to belong somewhere. Knowing he didn't made him feel ashamed. That's why when someone asked him, he let them think he was a runaway.

"My master," said Foxy, "he was a good man, I guess, but he just didn't want me no more. So I left."

Another stick snapped in two, and a whippoorwill's cry filled the lonely night.

"I'm—sorry."

Clay felt, suddenly, ashamed. He had so often felt sorry for himself, especially in those first days of winter when he realized how alone he was. Yet, he had Beauregard and Lazy Girl, and Clem in Washington City. Foxy didn't have a soul. Nor a place.

Clay knew now how important a place could be. He felt complete, whole, because he knew he would soon return to his beloved ridge in the mountains. He had his view of the clouds and the mists, and he had his sturdy cabin with its fireplace giving out cheer on cold nights. He belonged in the Smoky Mountains. He belonged on a special ridge, alike to many another, yet in so many ways his special place. He could never feel truly alone when he had his home. And he felt strong, just remembering it.

"Don't worry, Mister Clay," Foxy hastened to add.

"When I get to Washington City, where Mr. Lincoln is, everything will be fine."

Clay watched the fire leap and crackle. Then his eye caught something he hadn't noticed before. It was a handmade wooden spoon. It was made of white pine, and it had been scooped out with a whittling knife.

11

THE SUTLER had explained to Clay, back in the
Lynchburg camp, how the Reb entrenchments were laid out
around Petersburg. He told how the Rebs had constructed
earthworks and forts in a ten-mile-long line, from just east
of Petersburg on the Appomattox River, south in a huge
semicircle, then back up again to the Appomattox on the
west side of the city, where the boys were now.

Clay had heard about the basketlike objects, called gabions, which were often topped with sandbags, and the
chevaux-de-frise, or logs pierced by sharpened spikes, and
the fascines, which were small branches or twigs tied by
wire or rope into a bundle. He had learned from the sutler
that the chain of breastworks and artillery emplacements,
called the "Dimmock Line," protected all but the northern
approaches to Petersburg. He also knew that the fifty-five
artillery batteries were numbered, starting with "one" in the
east all the way to "fifty-five" in the west.

The Rebs had been dug in for almost a year now, and the
Billy Yanks were slowly, but surely, closing in with their
own huge encirclement.

When some field hands along the river told them they
were getting close to a Reb encampment, Clay figured they

were nearing the western end of the Reb line. He said to Foxy, "Reckon we'll start pullin' in to shore."

"Ain't we gotta meet up with them Yankees first?" asked Foxy. "The Doc, he say they making their own line, and breaking through the Reb 'trenchments!"

"They are," said Clay, "but they ain't reached this far yet."

"Hope you be right," said Foxy slyly. "If they start fightin', one of them minnie balls just might have our name writ 'cross it!"

Clay smiled, but he didn't feel too happy. He knew they would be in danger, and he knew it wasn't fair to ask Foxy to share the danger.

"Foxy," said Clay, poling the raft in to shore, "if you'd rather head north . . . go ahead to Washington by yourself, I can—"

Foxy cut him off with a vigorous shaking of his head. "If you got it fixed in your head to find that stubborn mule, I reckon I'll go along." He added, with a big smile, "I done took me a fancy to that critter myself!"

After they went ashore and scrambled up a steep bank, Clay's plan to skirt around behind the Reb line toward Petersburg was stopped by a gruff voice in a thicket.

"Halt! Who goes there!" A young sandy-haired Johnny Reb emerged, his bayonet threatening.

Clay and Foxy stood stiffly.

When they explained that they had come down the river and were looking for Clay's mule, the soldier narrowed his eyes and said, "I think I better take you to see the captain."

Clay shivered as they were led up over the sandbags and the sharpened stakes and stood looking down, for a moment, into trenches where huge gabions were stacked end on end. Soldiers atop the trenches turned sleep-reddened eyes to the boys, then turned back to glare into the distance.

The blue-clad troops would be out there somewhere—the noose of blue the sutler had talked about. It would be tightening from that direction. Clay could sense the tension, the bone-weariness, the deadening boredom. The endless waiting. And he could see the hunger in the hollow eyes and the sunken cheeks of the men.

Soon they were through the earthworks and fortifications and heading for a cluster of log huts squatting nearer the river. At last the soldier took them into one of the huts before a weary-looking captain. The captain was a handsome man with a trim black mustache. His eyes were hard, and when he questioned them his eyebrows, thick scraggly bushes, came together disapprovingly.

Clay patiently explained their problem, about how they had worked for a time for the sutler in Lynchburg, how they awoke one morning to find he had left with Clay's mule. In a faltering voice he told how he had overheard the sutler outside his tent talking about Petersburg. And how he was informed by the picket at Lynchburg that the sutler was last seen heading toward Petersburg.

"I think if we look, we might find him," said Clay. "Least I gotta try."

"I'm sorry," said the captain, tugging on the ends of his mustache, "but I can't worry about your personal property. You'll have to go back the way you came—if you can get back upriver. Thank God the Unionists haven't reached the river yet on this side. But the way they're cracking our lines and supply routes . . . the Boynton Plank Road . . . who knows, tomorrow it may be the southern railroad. They'll reach us here any day."

Clay remembered the sutler's saying how the Southside Railroad was the only rail line still held by the Rebs—the Rebs's only meager lifeline for food and materials to the impoverished city.

"But—we'd like to try," said Clay. "My Pa give me the mule and . . ."

The captain was studying a sheaf of papers in his hand, and he seemed not to be listening. He looked up, absently, as though he suddenly remembered the boys standing there. "What's that?"

"My mule . . ."

"I'm sorry, but if you boys don't want to get yourselves shot—"

"Maybe we could help here," suggested Clay desperately. "Like carry messages along the line or—"

"Sorry," said the captain. "Unless you're a trained—"

Just then a lieutenant at his elbow interrupted. "Begging the captain's pardon, sir, could I make a suggestion?" The lieutenant leaned over and whispered something into the captain's ear, and the captain tweaked his mustache and pursed his lips together thoughtfully. After a long silence he said, "Think you boys could learn how to make gabions and sap rollers?"

Clay's eyes questioned.

"Those things out there," the captain said, pointing through the hut opening to huge rolls of wickerware that resembled baskets. "They're used in the trenches and along earthwork walls to stop bullets," he explained. "And over there, beyond, those workers are making sap rollers. They're rolled to the head of a trench in progress to protect the workers from enemy fire."

"I think we could learn," said Clay.

Foxy nodded. "We could, sir."

"Tell you what," said the captain. "Those workers over there will show you how to make them. But, by God, you'd better keep in sight where we can see you. And if we start engaging the enemy, you boys'll have to retreat to safety. Don't want any boys on my conscience!" Taking in Clay's

105

long face, he smiled hearteningly. "You can talk to replacements as they come in, and couriers. Maybe you'll get some word of that merchant friend of yours." He laughed for the first time, showing a row of white healthy teeth. "Who knows, he may come right in camp here himself and plop that mule into your lap!"

Clay tried to smile too, and he thanked him.

Learning the work came easily to Clay, whose fingers had known basketweaving. Foxy, although awkward at first, learned quickly too.

For several days they worked, listening all the while to news about the war.

They learned that a recent attempt to capture Fort Stedman, the Unionist position near the City Point Railroad just east of Petersburg, had failed. They heard rumors of a big cannonlike weapon, a 17,000-pound mortar, being placed on a railroad flatcar to blast Petersburg from a distance of two and one half miles.

Clay wondered if that was the big "cannon" the sutler had talked about that evening outside their tent.

Listening and watching, Clay and Foxy learned also that the Confederate Army was losing its fighting spirit. Some even talked openly of deserting.

"I reckon," one of the soldiers was heard to say, "the only way to keep from starving to death is to desert to the enemy."

Clay knew that some of the men didn't take kindly to Bory's being in the camp. Clay was told there were not enough rations for the troops, much less for a hound dog. But he quickly explained that he would feed Bory from his own meager rations. Each night he went to bed hungry, Bory curled up by his side.

Of new arrivals, Clay always asked the same question—had they seen the sutler and the mule?

106

The answer was usually no, until one day a newly arrived corporal told of having seen a wounded merchant brought into camp at Fort Gregg, where he had served as a medic.

Clay felt his heart skip. He grabbed the soldier's arm and begged for more information. "Did he have a mule with him? A mule with a splotchy hide and she answers to the name of Lazy Girl?"

The soldier laughed. "Well, I wasn't proper introduced, but they was a sad-looking mule with him. We took her and put her in with the army horses."

Clay's hopes soared, and then he remembered that the soldier had said the sutler was wounded. "The man—" said Clay slowly. "Is he—"

"Was in pitiful shape when I left him," said the corporal. "Been hit bad. And he kept ravin' about how he had to get through to General Lee. Something about Sheridan and the Southside Railroad . . ."

"Southside! Why, that's what he said that night outside—" Clay swallowed a lump in his throat. "Did anybody believe—I mean, did the message . . ."

"Aw," said the corporal, "I don't reckon the medics paid any attention. Sounded to me like he was plumb crazy. Course," he shrugged, "might be one of the officers took down what he said."

I hope so, Clay prayed under his breath. Aloud he asked, "Where's Fort Gregg?"

The soldier seemed surprised at the question. "You ain't fixin' to go there?"

"Might," said Clay, "if we can get permission from the captain. Could you show me on a piece of paper?"

Clay ran to get writing material, and the corporal squatted on the ground and outlined the defenses and batteries for Clay, showing the location of Fort Gregg.

"See," he said, drawing the lines. "It's not too far from

Battery 45, and it's opposite the Unionists at Fort Fisher."
He rubbed a rough hand over his bearded chin. "Oh, I
reckon Fort Fisher's not three good miles away. Practically
aimin' their artillery down our gullets!"

Clay straightened. "I'm not afraid."

The soldier laughed. "Glad you ain't! I was danged glad
to get transferred here!"

Clay thanked the soldier and started off to seek out the
captain. He turned back suddenly. "Oh! Lazy Girl—she's
all right?"

"If that's her name, not a scratch, far as I could see."

Clay and Foxy stood again before the officer, whose
name they had learned was Captain Grey. "Captain Grey,
sir," Clay said in his newly acquired military manner.
"We'd like to request transfer to Fort Gregg."

The captain's eyes looked amused. "Transfer, you say?
Why, I thought you two were doing quite well here."

"We got word that the man we're after might be at Fort
Gregg. He's wounded and my mule is with him, sir."

Grey looked surprised. "Ah! You've caught up with the
rascal!"

"Could you give us papers for safe passage?"

The captain shook his head. "I don't know. That's not a
comfortable spot right now. If General Grant decides to—"

"We could help 'em make sap rollers, sir," said Clay
hopefully.

"Yes, suh," said Foxy. "We gettin' mighty practiced."

The captain smiled. "You're determined to get that mule
back, aren't you?"

"Yes, sir."

The officer reached for the quill pen on his desk. "Tell
you what. I'll give you passes to Fort Gregg."

Clay breathed deeply.

"But my advice to you is—find your mule and get back here with her as quickly as you can. If you're smart, you'll go back upriver and get out of this mess before it's too late."

Clay and Foxy departed from the camp with Beauregard. Clay felt sad saying good-by to the stern-faced but kindly captain. He knew the Johnny Rebs were desperate for fighting men—conscripting fourteen-year-olds for battle, even taking sixty-year-olds for the rear lines, yet Captain Grey seemed genuinely concerned about their safety. A kindly man, not too unlike his own Pa.

Along the line of grim defenses, Clay showed their passes to men in charge. Usually they were stopped by advanced pickets and led into a camp or fort where some officer looked at the papers, questioned them, then let them go. They had slim rations in their haversacks, and more than once on their journey Clay hankered for a place to fish, or a place to trap. He still carried his flintlock, but there was no game to be seen.

When they reached Fort Gregg, Clay saw that it was like many such forts that surrounded Petersburg. It looked to be about two acres of cleared ground, the front part on a rise looking down over an expanse of lower ground. It was surrounded with earthen embankments supported by legs and sharpened stakes directed at the enemy. Wicker baskets and sandbags were placed on the fortifications.

As Clay and Foxy came up alongside the fort, they saw that entrenchments and bombproof earthworks were in the rear, also a number of wooden huts. It had been raining for the past several days, but now, on this first day of April, the sky was bright blue and wispy white clouds floated overhead like scarves.

The sentries guarding the rear embankment looked at

Clay's passes, then took them before an officer in charge of one of the batteries, a major, who read their papers solemnly.

"You mean," he said after a while, "you came all this way just to collect a mule?"

"Yes, sir," said Clay.

"Do you have papers of ownership?"

Clay shook his head. In his pocket was a piece of chawin' tobacco he had got from one of the men back at camp. Lazy Girl, if indeed it was Lazy Girl, would head for his pocket where she knew he always kept some treat for her. But he realized that this might not be considered proof on the part of the Confederate Army.

The officer called one of his men. "Take these boys to the corral and see if that mule is the one they're after." He turned to Clay. "But you'll have to convince the lieutenant in charge there."

Clay finally asked the question preying on his mind since they had left the last camp. "The sutler, sir, is he . . ."

The officer shook his head slowly. "Is he a friend of yours?"

Clay nodded, hoping for the best, but fearing the worst. Something about the man's expression told him even before he spoke again.

"I'm afraid his wounds were too great to sustain. He died yesterday morning."

Clay sucked in his breath.

"We buried him in the southwest corner of the fort."

Clay fought to hold back tears. That day when he had lain in the road where he had sprained his ankle, he had looked after the Doc and in his heart cursed him for what he had done. Yet, all this while that he and Foxy were hunting for him, Clay hating him for stealing his mule, he still

110

held a grudging admiration for the strange peddler with the mixed loyalties.

Seeming to sense Clay's feelings, the officer continued. "He claimed he had a message for General Lee, something about a planned attack on the Southside Railroad above Five Forks."

Clay said, "I thought he had information he wanted to pass on—"

"He was a good man," said the major. "True to the Southern cause."

Clay swallowed hard, and a tear trickled down his face. He kept thinking about what the Doc had told them about loyalty having no place in the scheme of things. But he had been loyal, after all. The Unionists must have known what he planned to do and fired on him as he came through their line.

"The message," said Clay. "Did it get to Lee?"

"Yes. We didn't know if his facts were authentic, of course. But we sent it through channels."

Clay sighed. The Doc would have been proud.

At the corral Clay looked eagerly for Lazy Girl. In a moment, he spotted her among the other animals. She was chewing hard and she was muddy. She looked like the hind wheels of bad luck.

She would be all of twelve years old, and her hide was splotchy and her hocks were spavined. But she was his and his heart swelled with pride. He climbed through the fence to her.

"Girl!" he called softly. "Lazy Girl!"

The mule swished her tail and turned to stare at him. Then, in a twinkling, she was at his side, nudging his ribs affectionately and braying her welcome.

"Lazy Girl!" said Clay. "Did you miss me? Hey, don't nudge me so hard! You'll knock me over!"

The lieutenant in charge talked with the men sent from the major's hut, then turned to Clay. "How do we know this is your animal?" he asked. "She seems friendly enough to you, but—"

At that moment Lazy Girl nudged Clay's pocket, where he had the tobacco. She worked at the pocket with her teeth until at last she had the treat. She munched on it, contentedly, nudging Clay in the ribs when she had finished.

Clay turned to the sergeant who was in the corral with the horses. He was an old-timer whose red face and creased, weathered neck told Clay he was probably a farmer, like himself.

"Do you have tobacco in your pocket, Sergeant?" asked Clay.

The sergeant pulled on red suspenders and nodded.

"Did this animal ever try to take it off you?"

The old fellow's eyes crinkled merrily. "No, don't reckon she did."

"Well," said Clay triumphantly, "she knew I had some for her. I always keep a little treat for her in this pocket and"—his eyes were imploring now—"you saw how she came for it, right away!"

The lieutenant did not answer for several seconds. He watched them, boy and mule. At last he said, "I don't know. That's a lot of good horse meat for our hungry troops, sorely needed . . ."

Clay almost choked on his anguish. "*Horse meat!* You can't mean . . . This mule's a plowin' mule! She'd not—" Tears, hot and salty, streamed down his face and he made no pretense of wiping them away.

The officer looked to the sergeant and asked, "What do you think, Sergeant Hollingsworth?"

The old-timer looked away. Clay knew in his heart he was weighing the need for food in the fort with his apparent love of animals.

"I don't know, sir. I've got an ornery old mule back home in Biloxi. She's like family."

The lieutenant stood without moving. He looked again to Clay and Lazy Girl. Then he glanced toward Foxy, who was kicking a bit of straw with the toe of his boot, eyes downcast.

"If you had any other means of identifying . . ."

"Wait!" said Clay. "I know how I can prove she's mine! Could you bring her outside the corral for a minute? I'll show you!"

"Sergeant," said the lieutenant. "Bring that animal out here."

The sergeant grabbed Lazy Girl's halter and brought her out through the corral gate to where the lieutenant was standing. Clay slipped back through the fence.

"My Pa was visiting this foundry once," said Clay, "and Lazy Girl backed into a red-hot chain link. It burned into her rump, leaving a mark."

The officer raised his eyebrows and watched while Clay brushed the mud from the animal's rump. "If it's still here," said Clay. "Wait! Yes! There!" He pointed to a figure-eight mark on the hide of her hindquarters to the right of her tail. "You can still see it—plain!"

The others bent close to look and finally the sergeant said, "It's there, all right—just like the boy says."

Clay, Foxy, and Sergeant Hollingsworth all looked to the young officer, awaiting his answer.

The lieutenant finally shrugged. "All right. It looks like she's yours." He turned and started from the corral. "I'll re-lease her to you. I'll get our commanding officer to sign the papers."

113

Happiness, pure and sweet, washed over Clay like a welcome shower.

He buried his head in Lazy Girl's shaggy mane, inhaling the sweet, familiar, sweaty smell of her hide. He held her fiercely around the neck and said, "You ain't never gonna get away from me again. Never."

12

THAT AFTERNOON about four o'clock a rumbling was heard in the distance.

Troops strained questioning eyes to the hills and over the vast stretch of land that fell away from the fort to the southwest. Clay, readying his pack for their departure on the following morning, stopped his work and listened. He looked out over the abatis stabbing the sky to the death-still land beyond. The sun lingered on the green hills and a lone tree cast its skinny shadow on the earth.

"What is it?" asked Foxy at his elbow. "What you think them Yanks is up to?"

Clay shrugged.

"Don't know," drawled a corporal who was sewing a hole in his socks, "but I ain't gonna go out there to find out."

The corporal's friend, a red-faced sergeant, listened a moment before he returned to cleaning his rifle. "Might as well take them new shoes off that Billy Yank right now," he laughed.

"I need me some new underwear," laughed another.

The distant rumbling continued, but Clay decided from the laughter and good-natured talk that the sounds were too far away to be important. He returned to his pack.

Like troops in the last camp, the men here were badly clothed and hungry, but their spirits seemed high.

There was one private who had made himself a kind of crude Jew's harp out of discarded pieces of tin. He would go from campfire to campfire playing "Gay and Happy" while the men, some of whom were badly weakened from fever or dysentery, would try to shuffle their feet and dance.

Clay was warmed by the spirit of comradeship among the men guarding the fort. And he marveled at their energy. It seemed that someone was forever out beyond the front parapet, digging new trenches with bayonet and shovel and mess kit, replacing collapsing earthen walls, refortifying with sharp-pointed stakes, honing bayonets, greasing the axles on one of their two proud cannons.

After about two hours of the distant booming, sunset painted the skies a brilliant orange-red, then darkness crept over the fort. Campfires winked comfortingly over the vast fort area. Then came a strange silence.

The silence was almost unnerving. The silence seemed to Clay, suddenly, more threatening than the distant battle noises. It stirred in him a homesickness and a feeling of loneliness he could not still.

"You know, Foxy," he said to his companion while stroking Bory's long warm ears, "I reckon we're gettin' closer to Washington City, but it sure seems like it's a far piece right now."

Foxy, leaning back against a wagon in the rear of the fort where the hospital was located, sighed mightily. "It do seem a ways," he admitted.

Beauregard stood up and sniffed the air.

"What is it, Bory? Why you takin' on so?" asked Clay.

Foxy laughed, his strong white teeth pinkish in the fire glow. "Reckon he done sniffed him some hardtack one of them pickets is frying out there."

Clay rubbed Bory's protruding ribs. "Poor Bory, I know you're hungry, boy. So am I." He stretched out on the cold, still-damp ground and gazed longingly at the stars winking in the heavens. The stars looked so white, so clean washed, it made him think sharply of the stars that shone on his ridge back home. "Don't worry, Bory," he said sleepily. "We'll be leaving in the morning. Maybe we'll find you some game along the river . . ."

Suddenly an eerie whining split the night air. Clay jerked upright.

Behind them a shell burst with a mighty sound. Clay looked just in time to see a squirt of fire and mud and shrapnel flying skyward.

"Dear God," moaned a nearby soldier. "They're attacking!"

Another shell followed on the heels of the first, exploding in midair just short of the fort to fling shrapnel in all directions. One of the men in a forward position screamed, and Clay knew he had been hit.

The fiery red and orange explosions and the stench of powder that burned in Clay's nostrils filled him with the first real, cold fear he had known.

It was unlike the fear of facing a mountain lion or some other critter. It was unlike fighting for the way in a blinding snow blizzard or fording a treacherous stream. This was man-made danger, and it paralyzed his limbs and caused his heart to freeze. The stricken man's screams filled Clay's ears, and then were added the shouts and orders to troops about him.

"Get to your posts! Man the artillery! Hold your fire! Get that ammo out here! Where are the medics?"

A captain screamed orders hoarsely over the din, confusion, and shrieking of airborne shells overhead, the deafening explosions of the deadly projectiles and the mighty belch of flame from artillery at Fort Fisher.

There was general agreement among the men that the Unionists were closing in, tightening their noose . . . softening up the earthworks and breastworks along the line . . . moving up cannons, mortar too . . . lobbing death-packed shells into the very streets of Petersburg behind them.

Clay felt in his bones that this was the beginning of the end for that proud Southern lady, Petersburg, already on her knees after ten months of bloody siege. The shrieking shells and rapid explosions spoke of death and destruction and eventual surrender.

Clay knew the men must feel this too. Yet, strangely, every man of them from the commanding officer down to the drummer boy seemed to tense their fighting muscles. With the promise of death upon them, they seemed willing, even eager, to give their all if necessary.

After a long while, the enemy artillery was quiet. Clay and Foxy were called into the emergency aid station set up in the hospital, a long wood hut that had in its center a pot-bellied stove where boiling water steamed and hissed. Cots lined the walls and oil lanterns glowed eerily on the strained, whitened faces of the wounded as they were brought in on stretchers. A doctor worked feverishly to stem the flow of blood and bandage shrapnel-slashed arms and legs.

One man, a private who looked not more than nineteen or twenty, had caught a piece of shrapnel in his neck, and blood from the severed vessels transformed his gray shirt to red and soaked the stretcher on which he lay. The doctor quickly retrieved the shrapnel—a piece of iron embedded deeply—and determined that the wound had not severed a main artery. He gave the man a mild opiate and sewed up

118

the gash as best he could. Then he directed Clay to keep cold compresses against the wound. Foxy ran to and from the water barrel and helped stretcher-bearers find space for the new patients.

Clay and Foxy worked for hours in the hospital, not stopping to think about what was happening. They quickly bathed flesh wounds with water, applied cold compresses, applied tourniquets, tore up anything that could be used for bandages, kept water coming from the well, and boiled bandages.

The stench of blood and ether became almost overpowering. After a while, the doctor wearily told them they could be relieved for a time.

Up beside their own campfire again, Clay and Foxy wiped sweat from their brows and fanned them to a blessed coolness. They inhaled deeply of the fresh, crisp night air.

Presently a courier arrived with news that Sheridan's cavalry and Warren's infantry had attacked that afternoon at Five Forks, a Confederate-held position about fourteen miles southwest of Fort Gregg.

Clay clutched Foxy's arm. "The thundering today in the distance . . ."

Foxy nodded mutely.

General Pickett had fought bravely with only about 11,000 cold and hungry Confederates against an onslaught of more than 53,000 Northern cavalry and infantry, but at dusk Five Forks had fallen to the enemy. Part of the troops had tried to reassemble some miles north at Southside Railroad, but were defeated there. The grim defeat was told by the courier and later by men from Colonel Harris' Mississippi Brigade and from General Wilcox's Division, who gravitated to the fort and stayed, determined to fight it out there.

Through the night the men at Fort Gregg waited grimly.

They were now about five hundred men, but they knew there must be untold thousands of Billy Yanks out beyond the pale moonlit parapets.

The silence continued and finally, after the moon had moved across the heavens and night insects had ceased their music, a deathlike pall came over the waiting men.

A message reached the fort in the chill early morning hours that General Lee wanted them to hold the fort as long as possible, to fight a delaying action so that he and his troops could plan an escape to the west from Petersburg.

The plan was to hold the inner line of defense along Indian Town Creek, just behind Fort Gregg, until nightfall, when an orderly retreat could be made.

Clay found Sergeant Hollingsworth and asked what would become of the troops at the fort.

"The Lord only knows," said the Mississippian. "But," he added, snapping his suspenders as he had that morning in the corral, "we'll give 'em a danged good fight for General Robert E. Lee!"

Back in the rear of the fort, near the ambulance wagon, Foxy and Clay squatted over their small fire and talked earnestly of their innermost thoughts.

"Foxy," said Clay, "from what everybody says, they's gonna be some real fireworks in the morning." He swallowed a lump in his throat and continued. "I want you to . . . if you make it to Washington City and I don't . . ."

Foxy shoved back his red woolly cap and nodded. "I know, Mister Clay—you wants me to look up your brother."

"Yes."

"If you make it to Washington City," said Foxy thoughtfully, "and I don't . . . would you thank Mr. Lincoln—for my Granny?"

Clay was surprised. "But she's—I mean . . ."

Foxy smiled softly. "My Granny, she was a powerful thankin' woman. She wanted me to thank Mr. Lincoln for what he done for my people. You see, I promised."

Any other time Clay would have scoffed at the idea. But he nodded solemnly and said, "I'll try."

They waited there by the ambulance wagon and listened. The silence was now almost electric. Clay could hear the men breathing heavily all around him, and the moon had dipped down near the horizon.

"Foxy," he said at last, "I want you to know—I mean, I didn't count on gettin' you into this—"

"I wanted to come," answered Foxy. "You ain't noways to blame."

"You scairt?" Clay finally asked.

Foxy nodded. "I'm so scairt, my stomach, she feels like she was dropped all the way down in my boots."

Clay laughed nervously. He felt some better. At least he was not alone in his fear. He resolved that whatever lay ahead, he would perform bravely. His Pa would be proud.

13

IT WAS NEARLY FIVE O'CLOCK in the morning when a burst of gunfire from Fort Fisher awakened Clay and Foxy. They jerked up from where they were sleeping beside the ambulance wagon and rubbed their eyes.

"That's it!" barked Captain Charles Creager. "That's their signal for attack!"

Clay looked into the distance and saw the white glare from the signal fall into the fog-shrouded dawn around the Unionist fort.

At first nothing could be seen or heard in the mist sea beyond the parapets. Around them, men hurried to posts and fetched black powder for cannon charges. Officers rode their mounts up and down the earthwork lines yelling orders. The artillery teams began sponging the huge cannon muzzles and checking the planks on which the iron monsters had been placed over mud. Cartridge boxes bobbed wildly as the men ran about the fort, and nervous troops bit open ammunition loads, holding Minié balls in their teeth while they poured in the black powder.

At last all was in readiness. Men aimed their rifles over the front parapet in a neat row, like soldiers of tin that some child had placed there.

Clay and Foxy were told to stand by at the aid station. Earlier, they had torn bandages from old blankets, shirts, trousers—anything they could find for emergency use—and Foxy had chopped extra wood and refilled the kettle of boiling water atop the potbellied stove in the aid hut. The doctor and his medics waited with stretchers.

Still all was quiet.

At last the fog started to part like a curtain, revealing a long skirmish line of blue, moving toward them. Clay gasped when he saw their number. The distant hills, which had been quiet and motionless, were now swarming with uniforms. The uniforms were black in the early light.

A soldier cried, "Here they come!" and Captain Creager shouted, "Hold your fire till they're in range!"

Out of the gray morning came the line of running men, shouting their battle cries and holding high their regimental flags. Firing and swinging their rifles at all angles.

Artillerymen Don Cyrus and Bob Dickson of D Battery stood watching with steadied eyes and hands, waiting to jerk the lanyards on the cannons. Muskets were held at shoulder level. The blue line moved closer, and presently Clay could see men's faces, white in the pale light, and behind the skirmish line appeared two more support lines moving up.

"Fire the cannons!" came the hoarse cry of the captain.

The cannons suddenly became monsters belching fire and flame. The explosions almost deafened, and Clay believed he could hear echoes miles away. When the black smoke cleared, he peered into the advancing line and saw that many men had dropped where they were hit. But the main force came forward.

Artillerymen fed more powder into the hungry muzzles, rammed home the loads, then pushed in projectiles. They fired and fired again, each time dipping their long spongers

123

into water buckets and plunging them into smoking muzzles.

The order was given to return rifle fire. Into the faces of the enemy troops the men in gray poured deadly volleys from behind their earthworks and line of spiked abatis.

The skirmish line was repelled, and Clay saw flags trail to the earth, only to be picked up again by the second wave of attackers. Wave after wave of men in blue. Onslaught after onslaught.

Finally, the spiked logs were rolled aside, carried by main force, and tossed into the ditches. And then there were men grappling in the early light, stabbing with bayonets and clubbing with rifle butts.

The cries and moans of the wounded mingled with the cannon fire and sharp reports of a thousand rifles. The defense lines so perfectly formed were now ragged, and officers screamed over the din, "Fill those gaps!"

Torn bodies began to come on stretchers in a dreary, steady stream. Clay and Foxy worked in a fever pitch at their post. They helped carry wounded on stretchers, they boiled water and kept bandages handy. They applied tourniquets and slit open trouser legs for the doctor and medics. They cleaned dirt and grime from flesh wounds and helped administer opiates to those in most pain.

Clay and Foxy helped the doctor apply splints to a young Reb who had a smashed leg. The sight of reddened bone sticking grimly through the flesh caused Clay to blanch, but he wiped perspiration and dirt from the soldier's face and tried to offer words of encouragement.

Foxy, too, talked to the wounded in soothing tones, trying to cheer them.

There was no time to be afraid. After the battle started Clay and Foxy found themselves a part of a giant machine set in motion. The men out front, firing their rifles, worked mechanically too. The rifles, once loaded, were jerked to the shoulder and fired without apparent aim into the smoke.

The battle gained in intensity with the full light of morning. The sun glinted off bayonets in the distance, turning them into thousands of winking lights. A blue-clad corporal, hit in the stomach, crawled toward his regimental flag, and a bayonet served to pin him, forever, to the red-soaked earth.

Men fighting on the parapets crumpled grotesquely when hit, falling to the flat ground below and staring open-eyed and unseeing at the brightening sky.

Running with stretchers in zigzag lines to avoid the whizzing, whining Minié balls, Clay and Foxy felt the promise of death with each desperate step.

They strained under their awful loads, and once a grenade whizzed near. Clay grabbed Foxy's arm and pulled him to the ground seconds before it exploded and spewed its shrapnel skyward.

Mud-splattered and weary, Clay looked again and again to the parapet and saw that, despite the outnumbering onslaught of blues, the grays were, miraculously, holding the fort.

After a while there was a lull in the wave of attackers. A regrouping on a far hill gave the Rebs a chance to breathe freely for a spell. Orders were given for a company of men to proceed with haste to Battery 45, just behind the fort, to help man the line of inner defenses forming along Indian Town Creek.

"They've asked us for troops," said Sergeant Hollingsworth, coming up beside Clay. "They want all the men we can spare. Talked to Captain Creager about you—he's ordered you to go along."

Clay looked at his friend from the horse corral. He hardly recognized him at first. His face and hands were grime-streaked, and one red suspender was flapping about his burly waist. His kepi hat had been knocked askew, and he tried to right it while he yelled impatiently, "Don't stand there gaping. Get your mule and get goin'!"

Clay hesitated, "We're—helping here . . ."

"If you wanna' help, drive that ambulance wagon they're loading over there." He pointed to a group of stretcher-bearers lifting wounded into two wagon beds. He looked back to Clay and Foxy. "Can you drive a wagon?"

"I can," said Clay.

"All right. You drive that second one. Hitch that mule of yours in front of the lead horse. And you"—he looked to Foxy—"you can ride in the wagon bed with the wounded."

Clay did not answer for a moment, and the sergeant shoved him impatiently. "You're slow as molasses. Get that ornery mule and skedaddle!"

It came to Clay what the sergeant was trying to do. He wanted them to get away from the fort before things got worse. He wanted to protect them. Clay felt grateful, but words of thanks would not come.

Clay found Lazy Girl and hitched her to the front of the second hospital wagon. Foxy found Bory and lifted the dog into the wagon bed.

When Foxy had scrambled aboard and all were set to go, Clay reached out his hand to the sergeant. The sergeant took it firmly. "You're a fine lad, a credit to your family. Got a boy like you at home."

Clay felt a lump big as a Minié ball in his throat.

"Listen," said the sergeant quickly, "when you get these men to a field hospital—they'll tell you where when you reach the battery—you just . . . skedaddle." His voice became low and almost pleading. "You hear? You and that kid, you just skedaddle!"

Clay blinked back a tear. "Thanks, Sergeant." The lead

126

wagon jerked forward, and Clay grasped the reins in his hands. "Good luck!"

"God bless you," called the sergeant after them.

The new assault began almost as soon as the creaking wheels of the wagon bore them out of the fort at top speed. Clay looked back quickly, but the sergeant was hurrying away to his post near the front parapet.

At Battery 45, they were directed to a field hospital on the outskirts of Petersburg. The hospital was a building that held long rows of cots, most of them filled. Clay and Foxy helped place the wounded from Gregg in the empty cots. When there was no more room, they lifted them gently onto the bare plank floor.

Doctors and medics worked over the soldiers. There was much speculation about the retreat that would take place that evening from the city. It was planned to evacuate as many of the wounded as possible. Those too sick to be moved would have to stay behind. Doctors believed that, Reb or Yank, the sick would be cared for properly.

"Hey," joked one of the sick, "leave me behind. I'll get full rations for a change!"

Clay and Foxy helped the medics until they were no longer needed. At last Clay said to Foxy, "I reckon we'll be headin' on, like the sergeant said . . ."

Foxy silently agreed.

Into the town of Petersburg they went, riding Lazy Girl, while Beauregard trotted alongside. The streets, torn and ravaged by war, were still beautiful. There were lovely brick and frame houses, churches with tall white steeples, wide tree-shaded streets, and beyond, the Appomattox River catching the reds and golds of a breathtaking sunset.

Men, women, and children hurried here and there, preparing to leave the city. Many of the nonmilitary, apparently of a mind to stay in their homes, sat on porches and watched or peered from windows. Troops and wagon trains filled the streets.

Clay learned that General Lee had decided to take from the city the Second and Third Corps and General Field's Division of Infantry, the field artillery, and the long, long wagon train.

Clay knew the roads out of Petersburg would be badly rutted with mud from recent rains, and he marveled that the thin, underfed horses could pull the loads that had to be moved. The retreat, as it was said everywhere, would only be as strong as the horses' legs.

Not long after nightfall, the retreat got under way. Clay and Foxy watched from the doorway of a deserted building. The building, a handsome brick structure, was still sturdy, but many of its windows were broken, and there was a gaping hole in one side where a cannon ball had struck. When the artillery and troops in long, long lines started to move past, Clay felt an indefinable sadness. The departure was so different from the battle scene he had witnessed earlier. The cannons were now mute, and there were no screaming orders, no battle cries. Just a grim, almost silent display of defeated men marching with dignity along the city streets and across the Appomattox River.

After eight o'clock in the evening the guns were withdrawn from the city. General Field's Division had quit the feeble defense on Indian Town Creek, and those units of the Third Corps that had not been captured or driven westward along Hatcher's Run moved out as part of Longstreet's command. To Gordon was entrusted the command of the rear guard. He rode boldly, and Clay felt proud when he saw his dignity.

"What happened at Fort Gregg?" Clay asked any soldier

128

he could stop for a moment. No one seemed to know. Finally he stopped a corporal who limped behind the rest on crutches.

"Please," begged Clay, "do you know what happened to the men at Fort Gregg?"

The soldier nodded. "Most of 'em dead," he said, "or wounded. Some got away."

"How many were left?" asked Clay.

The corporal shook his head. "Don't know for sure. Some say twenty men—some say more."

Clay learned later that only thirty men were left unhurt at Gregg when, in the afternoon, it finally surrendered. Their delaying action had accomplished what General Lee wanted. It had enabled the general to make the withdrawal from Petersburg.

Clay wondered if his friend, Sergeant Hollingsworth, was one of the survivors. The thought that he probably would never know filled him with anguish and made his heart heavy.

As the last wagon pulled out of the city, its wheels creaking beneath its burden, Clay sighed and turned to Foxy.

Foxy's eyes said something of what Clay was feeling. He opened his mouth to speak, but only shook his head sadly.

It was quiet and dark in the city. A lamplighter made his lonely rounds, lighting a few streetlamps, and from a few houses yellow lamplight could be seen at the windows. Clay and Foxy, realizing they were too exhausted to travel any farther that night, curled up in the doorway to sleep. Morning would undoubtedly find Yankees swarming over the city, but that could not be helped. They wore no military uniform. Perhaps they would be left alone. It was a risk they had to take.

Clay was awakened after a while by a low, distinct

moaning. He got up and found his way to a nearby alley, where, in the pale light of a streetlamp, he could see a distraught soldier stretched out, one hand clutching a bullet-torn shirt.

He awakened Foxy. "Quick," said Clay. "They's a soldier hurt. He needs help."

They covered the soldier with their one remaining blanket and looked about for something they could use to dress the wound, something with which to stem the flow of blood.

"No," moaned the soldier in a hoarse whisper, "it's—too late. Just gimme—drink—wa-ter."

Clay unfastened his canteen and held it to the soldier's parched lips. The soldier started to drink. In a moment his head dropped back. Clay bent to his chest and listened for a heartbeat. Finally when he could make out no sign of life, he looked to Foxy. "He's—dead."

A late, mournful church bell chimed far off on a hillside. It sounded strange there in the quiet predawn streets of the nearly deserted city. Somehow it seemed sadder and yet more beautiful than any sound Clay had heard that day. It came to him suddenly that it was Sunday the day of worship and prayer.

A soft breeze played over the streets, gently rustling bits of strewn paper along the brick paving and walkways. In the breeze, which was cool to his flushed face, was a promise of spring.

He held the soldier's head for a long time, cradled in his arms. At last he lowered it gently to the ground. He looked at the still features of the young Reb's face. He was young, not much older than his brother, Clem. He reminded Clay, too, of Pete, who had fallen at Chickamauga Creek.

The moon moved from behind a skudding cloud and played over the soldier's face. Moonlight and a promise of spring. Church bells fading off in the distance. And grim death.

A cry of anguish was stilled in Clay's breast. He quietly walked away from the dead soldier. He was too exhausted to feel or think. And he could cry no more.

14

NEWS OF LEE'S SURRENDER to Grant at Appomattox Court House was being shouted from the rooftops when Clay and Foxy reached Washington City. Clanging of bells spilled drunkenly from church steeples. Strangers hugged each other in the streets. Horses clamored over cobblestones, and children chased in happy circles before high-stooped houses.

Huge stone government buildings trailed gay paper streamers. Saloons banged their doors on every street corner, and livery-stable owners came out of their places of business to inhale the sweet smell of victory along with the ever-present smoke from woodyards. Ducks and chickens, unaware that the long struggle was finally ended, picked their usual way along Pennsylvania Avenue.

At last the boys stood, awed, in front of an iron paling fence that surrounded the White House.

"Dear heavenly Father, I thank you," breathed Clay from the bottom of his heart.

Hearing the joyous bells, which seemed to ring all over the city, he recalled the Sunday before, that awful night in Petersburg when Lee's men had marched across their pontoon bridges, burning them behind.

Clay let his thoughts drift, too, to that next morning when they had reached Richmond in the wake of thousands of blue-coated troops. There they had seen burned-out buildings, bricks and mortar strewn into the streets like the following of an earthquake. They saw piles of grim, glowing ashes and a blood-red river dancing beneath crumbling high-arched bridges.

The armory in Richmond, once the pride of the Confederacy, lay an empty gutted shell, still smoldering.

They were arrested for a time in Richmond and accused of being looters, but released when a lean-faced soldier with kind blue eyes believed them and spoke to his captain in their behalf.

Sergeant Dale Wick, who befriended them, showed them the road that led out of the city toward Washington. Hungry and tired almost beyond going, they prodded Lazy Girl until they were safely out of the war-torn, confused city.

Through the rolling hills of Virginia they had made their painfully slow way, fishing when hungry, sleeping beside campfires at night, begging hay from farmers, who gave them cold stares and sometimes hateful words. One woman had pursed her lips together angrily when she saw Foxy and slammed the door in their faces, muttering, "I don't talk to trash!"

Remembering what his Pa had warned, Clay unconsciously hitched up his pants and squared his shoulders.

"Move along, move along," called a gruff-voiced policeman dressed in blue who was now trying to keep the crowds from gathering in too great numbers before the President's home.

Clay saw the disappointment flicker in Foxy's eyes. He knew the boy dreamed of seeing the man Abraham Lincoln. That foolishness of his—wanting to thank the President for his Granny—couldn't he know that it would be impossible even to get close to him? Thank him, indeed!

Clay stopped, suddenly remembering that night at Fort Gregg when Foxy had told him his dream. They were waiting for the signal for Fort Fisher to begin its attack, and they were frightened. Foxy's dream hadn't seemed too strange then. There, waiting for death, nothing had seemed real, yet nothing had seemed impossible.

Clay tugged tiredly at the pack straps on his shoulders and wondered if he would be able to find his brother. There was so much confusion in the city, and there were so many people. He didn't know which way to turn. Suddenly, a handsome black carriage clamored by, and mud flew up from its wheels, spattering them.

"I reckon we be a sight!" laughed Foxy, looking down at their clothes.

"Yes," said Clay, smiling weakly.

Clay wondered how he would look to Clem, when he found him. He and Foxy had bathed in the river and boiled their clothes a few days before. But they still had rents and tears—their sewing needle and thread had been left behind at Lynchburg—and their boots were badly scarred, the soles worn to a paper thinness.

At once Clay wished Foxy were not with him. He wasn't sure how the friendship would look to Clem. He was noticing that Foxy looked even more pitiful than he had the morning Clay found him in one of his traps.

"I reckon," said Foxy, as though he were reading Clay's thoughts, "we done reached what we set out for. I reckon we soon be saying good-by."

Clay hated himself for the feeling of relief that washed over him. "I guess."

They walked over to a park across from the White House, Clay leading Lazy Girl, who seemed to be the only

134

member of their party unruffled by the noise and frantic movement around them.

"I reckon you'll find yourself a job," said Clay with forced brightness.

"Sure."

Clay was cut by the tone of Foxy's voice. It didn't seem fair! The boy had got himself into that trap—then he had sweet-talked Clay into coming along to Washington City. There was nothing in their bargain that Clay had to take him on forever. The boy wasn't his problem anymore.

"You *said* they was more jobs than you could shake a stick at!" said Clay. "Come on, we'll find you a job, then I'll go hunt for Clem."

Job-hunting was not easy. Up and down the cobblestones they went, ducking carriages and stepping aside for ladies with huge hoop skirts to pass. Clay thought the skirts made them look like life-size china dolls. They asked at livery stables, they asked in general stores, riotously open, with beer barrels and hanging geese to celebrate the war's ending. They asked at homes and boardinghouses—anywhere they felt Foxy had some chance of earning a few dollars.

At last, tired and hungry to a point of faintness, they sat on a curbstone and pressed their chins into their hands. A horsecar swayed down the avenue. Beauregard whimpered softly beside Clay, who absently stroked his ears. It seemed hopeless. The town was filled with people going from door to door, begging for work. Many colored women, with babies in their arms, were pleading to work just for food to feed their families.

Clay and Foxy sat on the unfriendly stone a long time, not talking, and then, all at once, a big woman dressed in men's rough clothes called out from a livery stable behind them.

"Hey, you! Boys! Give me a hand with these boxes!"

135

Clay and Foxy looked around to be certain she meant them, and they hurried to help. They stacked boxes against a huge wall outside the stable, next to an alleyway. When the last box was in place, the woman said, in a husky but friendly voice, "I'm Miss Em, owner of this here stable. Them boxes is heavy. You did right good for such skinny 'uns!"

The boys smiled and started to leave, but Miss Em called after them. "Hey! Not so fast! You didn't think I was gonna get your help for nothing, did you?" She brought out a pocketbook and withdrew some coins.

"We don't want pay, ma'am," said Clay, removing his hat and patting down a cowlick with the heel of his hand.

"We didn't do that much," said Foxy, turning his woolly cap in his hands.

"Sure you did!" she said, wiping a dirt smudge from her cheek. She pressed the coins into the boys' hands. "That lazy Johnny took off, and I can't find him when I need him!" She lifted the man's hat from her head, pushed back a stray strand of hair and jammed the hat back on. "Hey, how come you look so all-fired mournful, noways? Ain't you glad the war's over?"

"Course we're mighty pleased, ma'am," answered Clay. He explained that they were tired because they had traveled such a long way.

The woman rubbed the back of her neck with big square-ended fingers. In spite of her size and her rough clothes, thought Clay, she was right pretty. Her eyes were so very blue, like Clem's, and her hair black and shiny as a blackbird's wing.

"What part of the country you from, anyways?" she asked.

"Tennessee," said Clay. He told how he had come from

136

the ridge in the Smokies and how Foxy had come from even farther.

The woman, now sitting on an empty crate and motioning for the boys to sit too, slapped her thigh. "Now, you ain't telling the whole truth." She laughed. "Sure you ain't come all that ways on your own two feet!"

Clay nodded.

Foxy told her how it had been, walking part way along the railroad to Lynchburg, taking the raft to Petersburg, becoming a part of the fighting at Fort Gregg, finally riding Lazy Girl from Petersburg to Washington City.

"Whew-eeee," said Miss Em. "If you two ain't had you some times! No wonder you look so pitiful scrawny! And long-faced too! I think I could step on them faces of yours!"

"We been looking for work," said Foxy, "but they ain't any."

"Who says?" asked Miss Em.

"That boy who was here said—"

She pshawed them. "That no-good stable hand! He's fooled me once too often. I just might be able to use me a couple of boys to clean the stalls, feed the animals. Don't pay much, but you'd eat."

Foxy grinned.

Clay said quickly, "He needs a job, 'cause he's planning to stay in this city. But soon as I find my brother . . ."

"I see," said the woman. She looked to Foxy. "You got any muscles under those skinny arms of yours?"

"Yes, ma'am," said Foxy. "I'm *real* strong."

Miss Em smiled.

"Me and Clay," he went on, "we done helped carry stretchers, and we helped at this field hospital, and I carried big loads of wood that musta weighed—"

"All right," Miss Em interrupted. "I reckon you'll do fine. When you wanna start?"

137

Clay grinned. He knew the woman knew that Foxy wasn't too strong. Why, he was just a scuff of a boy compared with the strapping big boys and even grown men who would give their right arms for the job. Jobs were that scarce. Yet Clay could see in her eyes that she was not an ordinary woman. She possessed a tenderness, a kindness, an understanding for a need. Her rough clothes and talk didn't fool him any.

She was a strong oak in a storm.

Foxy's eyes misted with happiness, and Clay felt his own threatening to mist up too.

"Right now'd be fine," said Foxy.

"All right. I'll get you grub first. You don't look like you could lift a harness right now. Then I'll show you which stall needs cleaning first."

After eating with Foxy and their wonderful new friend, Miss Em, Clay stabled Lazy Girl, instructed Foxy to keep Bory for a while, and started out to find Clem.

He visited defense installations around the perimeter of the city, for the most part grim gray clusters of tents and wooden buildings, until at last he came to an important-looking building, where he was shown inside, down a long corridor to the office of Major Al Wolgast. The major, who was working late at his desk, was a tall dark-haired man with understanding eyes. He listened quietly while Clay explained that he was looking for his brother. The major got up at last, went to a big filing cabinet and hunted for a time. At last he turned to Clay, smiling broadly.

"Your brother—his name is Clement F. Gatlin?"

Clay's heart had jumped happily. "Yes, sir!"

"Lieutenant Clement F. Gatlin?"

"I—don't know, but it must be."

"Yes, I have his assignment here. He's stationed with B

138

Company in the Georgetown sector. Wait. He's got off-the-post quarters."

Clay's eyes questioned.

Major Wolgast laughed. "That means he's allowed to live off the military post when not on duty. Here, I'll write out his address for you."

Clay thanked the major and all but ran from the building. Quickly, he found Tenth Street, almost in the heart of the city. Trembling with excitement, he walked along, looking for the number on the paper clutched tightly in his hand.

The houses were linked side by side in rows, up and down both sides of Tenth Street. Rows of steps led up to huge front doors that usually held bold brass knockers. Lacy curtains hung at the windows.

Finally Clay's heart leaped. He found the number he was seeking. Slowly he walked up the steps, and at last his hand reached for the knocker. His heart stood still when he heard footsteps approaching.

A woman wearing a bright-colored cloth about her hair opened the door a way. She frowned.

"What do you want?"

"I'm looking for Lieutenant Clem Gatlin, ma'am. Does he live here?"

The woman continued to frown. "What do you want with him?"

"I'm his brother."

She opened the door to him, still scowling. "All right. Go up those steps. His rooms are on the third floor."

Clay stepped into a dark hallway. Odors of cabbage and strong lye soap came to his nostrils. "Thank you, ma'am."

"Don't know if he's in or not. Maybe his wife is."

Clay climbed the stairs that creaked beneath his feet.

"Please," he prayed softly beneath his breath, "let him be here."

On the third floor he saw brass plates with names on them affixed to two of the doors. He burned with anger at himself because he could not make out the writing. He hesitated at one door, finally knocking softly.

Heavy footsteps came toward the knocking. Clay stiffened. Suddenly he was filled with a nameless fear. What if Clem wouldn't be happy to see him? What if he had changed? What if his wife didn't like him? What if . . .

"Yes?" A man's face stared at him in the dim hallway light. It was a familiar face, yet strange and unfamiliar because of a square-cut beard. The face was strong-jawed, young, eyes set evenly apart, handsome . . . it was Clem!

Clay took a deep breath. "Clem?"

Clem, wearing a blue uniform, his sandy hair brushed to an unaccustomed neatness, looked puzzled for a moment. At last the muscles of his face relaxed into a big broad grin —a grin Clay had remembered and carried in his heart since he had gone away from home.

"Clay!" his brother boomed, blue eyes twinkling. "Clay! I'm a son-of-a-gun! Clay Gatlin!"

15

PAGES OF TIME magically leafed backward. Clay was suddenly nine years old and at the cabin again. Beauregard was whining to be after the scent of rabbit. He and Clem were getting their hunting rifles down from the smoke-blackened rack over the fireplace, and Ma was wrapping them up a piece of salt pork and six catfish-head biscuits.

They were together, Ma and Pa and Clay's brothers, and crisp fall air brought a scent of woodsmoke and chestnuts ripening in a far-off verge of wood.

He could almost hear the sounds, faint in his memory, yet clear as if it were right now. Pa talking to Lazy Girl out in the shed, and Little Davey squealing for Pete to play "horsie" with him.

"Clay," whispered Clem, breaking the wondrous spell. "It's *good* to see you!" Clem pulled him inside a parlor with ruffled white curtains and closed the door with a bang. "Danged if it ain't good!" He hugged him.

"Clem," said Clay, smiling broadly and forcing himself back to the present. "You're looking fine!"

"Mollie!" shouted Clem. "Come see who's here! It's my little brother!" He turned back to Clay, his eyes twinkling. "Did I say *little* brother? Lordie, how you've grown!" He

141

laughed and poked Clay in the chest. "Still skinny, though!"

Clem looked handsome as a tintype picture. He wore a fancy uniform that made him look like some general, and his beard, a kind of sandy-brownish color, was trimmed so neat it looked like a soldier Clay once saw on a package of fancy tobacco. His heart expanded.

"How did you get all the way here in Washington City? How's Ma . . . and Pa? Tell me, did Pa ever get over—"

Clay's eyes quickly sought the floor, breaking off Clem's questions. When he looked down he saw a pretty red pattern in the carpet. A soft silky rustling nearby told him Clem's wife was coming into the room. He kept his eyes on the red pattern, not looking up, not even at Clem's next words.

"Clay! *What is it?* Why ain't you answerin'?" His brother grabbed Clay's arm, digging fingers into his flesh. "Tell me!"

"I didn't aim to—" He looked up and saw that Clem's face had gone white. A blue vein twitched in his temple.

Clay was aware of a faint ticking of a clock in the room and the beating of the blood in his own temples. Outside, happy throngs of people celebrated.

"The fever took Ma," said Clay as in a dream. "And after her, little Davey . . ."

Clem sank to the dark-red horsehair sofa. "Dear God!" He buried his head in trembling hands.

"They was—awful sick," said Clay. "A lot of the neighbors come down with it too. Ma spoke of you before she—" Clay couldn't go on. "I hate to be the one to tell you, but, Clem, Pa's gone, too, in the war. Before Ma, even. And Pete was lost at Chickamauga Creek."

Clem looked as though he had been struck. He had such an awful hurt in his eyes that Clay wished he hadn't spoken.

142

Clem buried his head again in his hands, and then he spoke with a kind of heartbreaking, dry sobbing.

Maybe it was wrong, telling him right out. Clay had planned to tell him later, after they had talked a while. But maybe it was good it came out all at once. Bad news wasn't ever easy.

And there was no way to ease the hurt. No matter how much he loved him.

Finally, Clay was aware of Clem's wife, looking at her husband with the gentlest eyes, reaching out a hand to console him, but not quite touching him.

She was a smartly set, pretty little woman. She was small-boned and she had eyes like a gentle doe's. She had a way of looking at Clem that spoke of how much she loved him. After a while, she withdrew her outstretched hand and fingered a brooch holding some white lace at her throat.

Clem, finally noticing her standing there, said to Clay, "This is my wife, Mollie. Mollie, I'd like you to know Clay, my brother."

Mollie put a small, cool hand into Clay's big rough one and he shook it firmly. "Pleased to know you, ma'am."

"I'm happy to meet you," she said. "I'm so sorry about—" She broke off, quickly. "You two will want to talk. I'll fix something in the kitchen."

When she was gone, Clay said, "Clem, you look just fine. Little stockier." He tried to manage a laugh. "Being married must be—"

"Mollie's a wonderful girl," said Clem. "Clay, tell me, how did it happen with Pa?"

Clay forced himself to relive the terrible days after the fighting at Knoxville when Pa had come home wounded. He tried to keep the hurt from his voice, and he left out the part about how Pa cussed Clem and forbade them to speak his

143

name. He told, too, how it was with Pete at Chickamauga. How his buddies had sent letters saying how brave he was. And he told how the preacher came from the next ridge and said words over Pa, and later for Ma and Davey. He told how they were together there in the little plot out back of the cabin.

"I was hoping," said Clay earnestly, "you'd like to come back with me, now the war's over. Lazy Girl's here in Washington City with me. Bory, too . . ."

"Clay," Clem implored. "I've *got* to know. Did Pa ever forgive me for going off?"

Clay studied the carpet some more and tried to form the right words. It was his way to speak the truth, like Pa always taught him. But somehow he couldn't bring himself to do it now. He took a deep breath and said, hoping the Good Lord would forgive him, "Sure, Clem, Pa got over it. He forgave you."

They talked together there in the small, cozy parlor until the late hours. They relived old times—the good times—and spoke of old friends and neighbors. Clay told about John Brewster and how he had helped him with advice on plowing and planting. How Mr. Findlay had traded him money and food staples for fur.

At last Clem said, "It musta been hard for you, Clay, and mighty lonesome."

Clay smiled. "Sometimes."

"When I think about it," said Clem, "you there all alone on that ridge and winter coming . . ."

"I reckoned," said Clay, "that maybe you'd come back with me. We could work that land and maybe get an extra mule to help Lazy Girl." He laughed. "She's gettin' kinda old, and mighty persnickety! Maybe we could get some pigs and clear off that section down by—"

144

"Wait," said Clem, placing his hand on his shoulder. "I can't. I can't come back with you."

Clay felt a stab of pain.

"I—don't understand."

"Maybe," said Clem, "I once said I might come back, but"—he shrugged—"things is changed." He got up and walked across the room, looking down briefly at the busy street of celebrators. "I'm a married man now and I've got —well, responsibilities. You'll understand when you're older."

Clay must have let some of his feelings come into his eyes, because Clem said to him in a soft voice, as if he were explaining to a child. "Clay, you saw Mollie. She's such a little thing. Kind of frail. You think she could live up there? Fighting freezin' cold in winter and in summer helping with all the hard work and—oh, hang it all, Clay. You know how hard it is, squeezin' a living from that rocky land."

It was hard sometimes. Clay remembered his Ma hankering for pretty things, worrying herself gray and her hands getting red and rough. He couldn't picture Mollie there, no matter how hard he tried.

"Where would you go? What would you do?"

"Mollie's father—he's got a carriage shop in Baltimore. Makes wheels and such. It's a good business and he could use someone like me. He's offered me a partnership."

Clay couldn't imagine his brother living in a city, crowded in by people and brick buildings. "Is that what you're after?"

"Mollie wants it," said Clem. "And—I'd like to try it."

Clay could find no more words of persuasion. He knew it would do no good.

"Say!" exclaimed Clem. "What do you say you come to Baltimore with us and live with us?"

145

"I don't know."

"We're the only two Gatlins left," said Clem. "We gotta stick together now!"

"I—guess so," said Clay, still not sure.

"I tell you what," said Clem, grinning. "You stay here with us for a while, see how well we get on. We can fix you up a nice bed on this sofa—it ain't so bad—and Mollie's a danged good cook."

"Well . . ."

"When I'm discharged, we'll go to Baltimore and get us a house where we can keep Bory, and maybe even find a place to board Lazy Girl too!"

Clay looked to the dark window where Clem was now standing. Street noises drifted up. Clay got up and walked toward the sounds. Looking down, he could see people clear as day. Gaslight spilled over their faces, their smiles and their fancy clothes. Rigs and carriages sped past in the streets and voices rang to the sky in songs of victory. Across Tenth Street from Clem's rooms, there was an opera house and it sparkled with lights.

"That's Ford's Opera House," said Clem. "They're putting on a fine play there. Would you like me and Mollie to take you some evening, when you're rested?"

Clay had never seen a play, but John Brewster had told him about them. They were probably fine things. He supposed there were many fine things to see and do in the city. Yet, suddenly, the noises and the rushing, laughing people on the street made him realize how tired he was. How bone-weary, and how lonesome for home.

"All right," he said without much real enthusiasm. "If you'd have a mind to."

"And you'll go with us to Baltimore?"

"I'll think about that."

Each morning Clay awakened on the sofa and listened to the morning sounds of the city. The flagstone and wooden walks rang with the tempo of early-rising government workers. Teams of horses were snorting and pulling wagons, and Clay could hear drivers call to them. Whistles blew and sometimes church bells rang out, and he could hear the soft swishing of brooms as ladies up and down the street swept mud from their stoops.

It was good being with Clem. And Mollie was dear to him, treated him fine. Yet—he felt more and more boxed in by the city. He visited Foxy at the stable each day.

"Foxy," Clay said on Friday, "I've been thinking maybe I'll be moving to Baltimore with Clem and Mollie. They want me to live with them."

Foxy, oiling a harness, looked up, surprised. "You ain't going back to your home?"

Clay twirled a piece of hay between his fingers. "I ain't sure yet."

A pucker of concentration appeared between Foxy's eyes. "But you ain't no city boy. You'd not be happy."

Clay snorted. "You like the city. I can learn, I guess."

Foxy looked down and bit his lower lip. "But—with me, it's different. I ain't got no place—I don't belong nowhere like you."

Clay knew it was true. The only reason Foxy had wanted to come to Washington City was to be where Mr. Lincoln was.

"Have you seen Mr. Lincoln yet?" asked Clay.

Foxy shook his head sadly. "I go down every day to that White House where he lives, and I look and look everywhere, but I can't seem to—"

"Don't fret none," said Clay. "You'll get to see him one of these days."

"I hope so," said Foxy.

On Friday evening Clay attended early church services with Clem and Mollie. Mollie wore a pair of pretty white gloves and a lacy shawl that she pulled up around her brown hair. Clem wore his uniform and he had shined his boots until they gleamed like newly minted coins. They had bought Clay a new suit of clothes, and he twisted and turned in his pew, they felt that unnatural. And his new shoes pinched.

But the service was beautiful. There were shimmering candles alongside the altar and banks of lilies. Listening to the choir and thinking about the miracle of the rebirth, Clay got a lump in his throat. Dear Lord, he prayed silently at the end of the services, help me to know what to do.

Walking back to their boardinghouse, Clay saw a knot of people across at Ford's Theatre. He asked Clem and Mollie what was happening.

"They're hoping to get a glimpse of our President," said Mollie, smiling. "He and Mrs. Lincoln are attending the play tonight. It's supposed to be a very funny comedy with Laura Keene." She turned to Clem. "Dear, I wish we had got tickets."

"I did promise Clay we'd take him," said Clem. "But now that Lincoln's going, you ain't—"

"Wait!" said Clay. "Are you *sure* the President will be out there tonight?"

"Sure," said Clem. "He should be along any minute . . ."

"Please, you go on to bed without me," said Clay, rushing to change his clothes. "I want to find Foxy at the stable. In fact, I might stay the night there, so don't wait up for me."

"Well," said Clem hesitantly, "be careful."

Clay started back up Tenth Street toward the stables,

148

but in a twinkling he caught sight of Foxy's red woolly cap and his eager face, straining to see the carriages that came up alongside the theater. Clay was about to call out to him, when all at once a voice in the crowd shouted, "Here he comes—*Abe Lincoln!*"

A smartly outfitted coachman walked the horses down Tenth Street and stopped his coach grandly in front of the theater. Presently, a footman jumped down and helped the ladies from the carriage. Then the President alighted.

Clay froze. Foxy was pushing forward, as if to speak to the tall man. A policeman in front of the theater ordered him back. Clay knew what Foxy wanted to do, had to do, and his heart ached for him. Even if he could speak, his words would surely be lost in the murmuring of the crowd and in the stiff breeze that came up.

Clay remembered painfully what John Brewster had said. One grain of wheat in a whole wheatfield didn't cause much notice. No one noticed Foxy. But Foxy's eyes, even from where Clay stood, were plainly alive with yearning, as if candles had been lighted behind them. As if they were praying for a miracle.

And then the miracle happened. It was such a tiny miracle, really, and it happened in a flick of an eyelash. As a man in dark clothes walked a few paces with the President to the theater, the tall, majestic Lincoln with the deeply brooding eyes glanced toward Foxy. His glance seemed to be held for a moment by the small dark boy in the red woolly cap. And in those dark eyes there was all that Foxy felt in his heart—the thanks—and the big man called Abraham Lincoln seemed to see it. He nodded briefly toward the boy, and a small smile played over his lips.

Then he was gone inside the theater.

When Clay looked to Foxy again, he saw that tears were washing down his small elfin face.

16

THE CHANNEL, which flung its long arm inland from the Potomac River, glimmered eerily under a bright moon. The mist that had shrouded the city earlier like a cloak was clearing. A cool, stiff breeze blew. Clay, sitting cross-legged on the bank of the channel just below the Tidal Basin, pulled up his collar.

He felt a million miles away from home and more alone than he had ever felt before.

Idly he picked up some pebbles and tossed them into the water. The moonlight caught the ripples and made his hands a ghostly white.

He looked at the big, cold stars that hung over the water. They were so clear he felt he could reach up, pick a few as you would field daisies, and take them home to Clem and Mollie.

In the city he never noticed stars much. But here, near the water, they looked almost as close as they did from his ridge back home.

A yearning for home came over him. He thought how it would be never to sit on the cabin porch, looking at the little dipper and the big bear, Bory plopped beside him thumping the porch boards with his tail.

Earlier, when he had seen Foxy standing outside the theater, he had started to call to him. But somehow he had this need, strong and pestering, to be alone. He had started walking down Tenth Street, crossed wide Pennsylvania Avenue, and walked until he reached Constitution. At Constitution he turned right and walked to Twelfth Street. At Twelfth Street he turned left and walked over the wide grassy mall, then went on until he reached Maine Avenue, where he turned left and found the channel. He knew the names of the streets because Clem had taught him.

With each echoing footstep, with each lonely gaslight he passed, with every far-off moanful wail of an ocean-bound ship, he asked himself the same question: Should he go with Clem and Mollie to live in Baltimore?

Baltimore was a thriving city, a seaport town. Mollie had told him it was a grand place, with tall buildings and big ocean ships coming in and out. There were fine houses with lawns and wide streets. She said he would probably like it there. He knew he wanted to be with Clem more than anything else in the world. Clem said they would find a place to live where they would let Bory stay, and that maybe they would even board Lazy Girl in a stable.

Clay tried to imagine Lazy Girl living in a rented stable, growing fat and sassy, and himself visiting her whenever he could. He would probably get a job somewhere or help Clem in the carriage factory.

Who could tell? Maybe he'd learn to like city life.

He sighed and tossed two more pebbles into the water. It came to him, watching the widening ripples, that maybe their lives, his and Clem's, were now like those different circles in the water. That was Clem, that first circle, the bigger one. That would be Mollie's circle too, and someday their children's. And the smaller circle, that would be him and Bory and Lazy Girl.

151

Their circles might touch, but could they ever belong to each other?

He wished he knew what to do. Before leaving home, he had wanted Clem to guide him, to tell him what to do. Yet now he knew he had to decide things for himself.

He supposed that was part of growing up, deciding things alone.

He closed his eyes, trying to will himself not to think any more about it. But he couldn't stop his thoughts from tumbling.

He thought about Foxy. Foxy didn't really belong anywhere either. The only reason he wanted to be in Washington City was to be near Mr. Lincoln.

Clay knew he didn't hate Foxy anymore, nor blame him for causing the war. How different he had felt when he started out! What *was* the difference between liking and hating? Was it understanding? The answer echoed clear to his mind as if he had spoken the word aloud.

Yet, he thought sadly, I don't really understand myself. If I did, I'd know what to do now.

He finally got to his feet and started back uptown. It was colder now and he pulled his coat closer. When he reached Constitution and started toward Tenth Street, he stopped dead in his tracks.

The streets, usually asleep at this hour, were suddenly alive with people. And the people were hurrying past him, up Constitution Avenue and turning left on Tenth Street. Men and women were wild-eyed and some of the women dabbed at tear-streaked faces. Men were pouring out of the bars and hurrying, grim-faced, along the street. People talked to each other in hushed, excited tones, and Clay tried to hear what they were saying.

He passed a small boy, sitting alone on a curb, crying to himself.

152

"What's the matter, little feller?" asked Clay. "Why are you—"

"The President . . ." sobbed the boy, lifting a reddened face. "He's been killed!"

Clay gasped.

The boy started to tell Clay more, but just then his mother, a big woman wearing a flowered dress under a black coat, snatched him up and hurried with the crowds toward Tenth Street.

Lincoln killed! Clay felt it couldn't be true.

He had seen the President with his own two eyes, just a little while ago, walking into Ford's Theatre. Mollie said it was a funny play. Everybody was wrong. It was a mistake, and the President was still in the theater, watching the play and laughing his head off.

"That's what it is," said Clay, as though speaking it would make it true. But, even as he said it, he found his own feet hurrying with the others. He crossed Pennsylvania Avenue and he saw a big crowd in front of Ford's Theatre and a bigger knot of people across the street in front of a house next to where Clem lived.

"Lincoln's shot," whispered somebody near him.

"He's dead," said another.

"No," said another. "He's not dead yet."

"Don't you worry, honey," said a man to his distraught wife. "Nobody can kill old Abe Lincoln. That man's too tough. He'll be all right, you'll see."

Clay saw Clem and Mollie in the crowd before the house. Later he learned that the house belonged to a tailor, a Mr. Petersen.

"Clem," called Clay anxiously, "what happened? These people are saying—"

Mollie's eyes, misted with tears, told him it was true. Clem, squeezing her arm, said to his brother, "He was

153

shot by some crazy actor fellow while he watched the play. He's in that house." He pointed to a kerosine light flickering in a window. "They took him there and the doctors are with him."

"Mrs. Lincoln's there too," said Mollie.

Clem's face showed his sadness. "Clay," he said gravely. "He was a great man."

"Please," pleaded Mollie, her finger to her lips. "He's still alive. Maybe there's a chance."

Clay remembered some of the things people had told him about the President. He thought of how they said he was a kindly man. He remembered how they said he was born poor, and how he had split rails to buy law books. Mostly, he thought of what Lincoln had said at the Gettysburg battlefield. They were mighty stirring words, words that Mollie had read to him one day. They were words worth pondering.

Mollie had told him, too, what Lincoln had said about slavery. "As I would not be a slave," he said, "so I would not be a master."

That was worth pondering too.

Cavalry officers, riding snorting horses through the crowds, cursed loudly and tried to get the people to return to their homes. But as soon as the officers scattered one group, another group pushed in to take its place. The people stood there stubbornly in the chill wind waiting for news.

Clay thought of Foxy. Foxy wasn't there, and so he was probably asleep at the stable. He would be heartbroken when he learned what had happened.

Clay thought, too, of the President as he had seen him walking into the theater—of his deep-set, melancholy eyes in the craggy face.

154

It was a face that would always haunt him.

"Will he die?" asked Clay.

Clem shrugged. "Some say he will."

Clay shivered and sent a little prayer skyward. Others near him were praying too, because he could see their lips moving silently.

As they watched, a tall man in a black suit, carrying a briefcase, came from the Petersen house, shook his head and hurried to a waiting carriage. Another carriage pulled up to the house, and policemen and soldiers ordered the people to make a path.

Finally, some of the people who came from the house said the President was dying, that doctors could do nothing to save him.

At last Mollie and Clem decided to go inside their own rooms. They urged Clay to come along too. "There's nothing we can do now," said Clem. "Come on."

"I'll be along—later."

After Clem and Mollie had gone, Clay turned and walked toward the livery stable on F Street. He passed more people in the streets, all talking in hushed voices, some of them praying. Many of them were crying.

Everybody seemed kind of lost, stunned, as though they couldn't believe what had happened. But saddest of all were the freed slaves, the men and women, and the little children that clutched their mother's skirts and asked what was wrong. One mother, wearing a red kerchief about her head, was holding a baby to her breast and moaning softly, "Honey—our President's dying. What we gonna do? What we gonna do?"

It was like a chant, a lullaby of loneliness and desperation.

When Clay went around to the little shack in back of the

155

livery stable, he knocked softly. Miss Em came to the door.

Clay took off his hat. "Evening, Miss Em—have you heard about—"

The big woman nodded. "I sure have." She blew her nose with a big handkerchief. "Come on in, young feller. I tell you, that was a great man. This country's gonna go to the dogs without him to fix things between North and South."

Clay thought about this. It was probably truth. He had heard that Lincoln favored a soft treatment of the South, so there would be no bitterness. Now . . .

"Has the boy . . ."

"Don't reckon he knows yet," said Miss Em. "He come back here all shiny-eyed and grinning like a mule eatin' briers. Lordie, but that little 'un was happy, seeing the President with his own eyes!"

Clay sighed.

"He was gonna rest a spell," she said. "Then he was aimin' to go back to the opery house and wait till he come out again."

"Could I—stay a while?" asked Clay. "I'd kind of like to be the one to—tell him."

"Sure." She led the way through a small passageway to the stable door. "You can stay long as you want." At the door of the stable, she stopped Clay with a frown. "You know, I feel sorry for that little 'un. He's such a scrawny—" She wiped her nose again with the big handkerchief. "Fact is, I gotta get me another stable boy."

Clay froze. "You mean . . ."

"I don't wanna do it," she said, "but they's more work here than he can do by hisself. Oh, he tries—works like a regular tornado. Oh, hang it, I just gotta get me somebody bigger. You understand?"

"Sure, I understand."

"Mind you," she said quickly, "I ain't hardhearted, no,

156

sir! I'll not tell him right away. Not till I've had a chance to look around to see if there ain't someplace else he can get work."

"I understand," said Clay again. He had helped Foxy work and knew the boy could hardly reach the high-up boards where the harnesses hung. And he had seen him climb up on boxes to saddle a horse or to rub one down. He reckoned that when Miss Em had offered Foxy a job, she had figured on both of them working together. He was much taller than Foxy, and he could reach the high places.

Clay tiptoed quietly into the dark stable. A familiar odor of animals and hay and leather reached his nostrils. High-up windows let in some of the light from the streets, and the voices of the crowd drifted in like a soft murmuring. Or a funeral dirge.

But Foxy didn't hear any of it. He was curled up in a tight ball in the big loft, sound asleep. One hand was outstretched, and he breathed loudly. Clay looked at him for a while, at the soft light playing over his features. He sure was a scruff of a boy, all right. He looked like an elf, too, with that red woolly cap pulled down to his eyebrows.

Bory whimpered softly and Clay said, "Don't wake him, boy. Let him sleep."

He thought about the time in the cabin when Foxy had slept clean through a day and a night, and him and Bory sat waiting for him to wake up. He thought about how strange it had sounded there in the cabin, Foxy's breathing so loud, and how funny he had looked when he finally got into Clay's old clothes that hung loosely on his small frame.

Clay remembered, too, all the times they had had crossing country, getting to Washington City. There was that time Foxy saved his life when he had the fever. And the time he helped him carry stretchers in the battle at Fort Gregg.

And the sword. He looked over to where the boy slept, and in the dim light he half expected to see the sword there.

Foxy stirred and said, "That you, Clay? What you doin' here?"

"It's me, but you can go back to sleep."

"I can't," said Foxy, trying to get up and rubbing his eyes. "I gotta get back. I want to be there when he comes out again."

Clay laughed. "You done slept too long. The play's over and everybody's gone home."

Clay could sense the boy's disappointment.

"Don't worry, Foxy. You go on back to sleep. I'll stay here too. When you get up in the morning, I'll help you with your work."

"That's fine," said Foxy sleepily, and then he fell back in the hay and curled up again in a ball.

After a while, Clay listened to a steadier breathing that told him the boy was asleep again. No use telling him to-night. Bad news might be easier to take in daylight.

Clay curled up too, and Beauregard sidled up to him, between him and Foxy. Clay lay for a long time, patting Bory and listening to his big, friendly tail thumping in the hay.

And then Clay knew what he would do.

The answer came to him in such a simple way. It was as if the answer had been there all the time in his heart.

In the morning, after he would tell Foxy the news about Mr. Lincoln—telling him kindly as he knew—he would tell Miss Em they would help with the work until she could find somebody else.

He would ask Foxy if he wouldn't like to go back with him to Tennessee.

And he knew in his bones that Foxy would favor the idea.

Foxy learned fast. He was a mite small, as Miss Em said,

158

but Clay knew he could teach him how to plow and plant in a straight line and, with the help of him and Lazy Girl, to pull stumps.

In time he would get some meat on him and grow taller.

Clay sighed with satisfaction. It was like a great burden lifted off his shoulders, knowing what to do.

Just before falling off to sleep, Clay remembered how Foxy had said he never favored the name folks called him. Foxy didn't seem a fitting name for him, and that was a fact. What would he call him? Dan'l wouldn't do either. Foxy wasn't like Dan'l in that lions' den, not really. At that fort he had been just as scared as anybody. And he wasn't like Dan'l Boone, though Clay had to confess he was learning fast to be a mountain boy.

What name would he call him? As sleep made him drowsy, names kept flitting in and out of his head like cabbage moths. Oh, well, he'd think of a name tomorrow. Tonight, the only fitting name he could think of clearly was "friend."